W9-AYG-209

MYTH-O-MANIA
IV

UNDERWORLD LIBRARY
ANCIENT GREECE

AUTHOR
Kate McMullan

TITLE
Nice Shot, Cupid!

DATE DUE	BORROWER'S NAME	
XXVII	Lord Hades	
XXXI	Lord Hades	

Myth-O-Mania is published by Stone Arch Books
A Capstone Imprint
1710 Roe Crest Drive,
North Mankato, Minnesota 56003
www.capstonepub.com

Text copyright © 2012 by Kate McMullan

All rights reserved. No part of this publication may be reproduced in whole or in part, or stored in a retrieval system, or transmitted in any form or by any means, electronic, mechanical, photocopying, recording, or otherwise, without written permission of the publisher.

Library of Congress Cataloging-in-Publication Data is available on the Library of Congress website.

Library binding: 978-1-4342-1985-5 · Paperback: 978-1-4342-3435-3

Summary: Hades lets readers in on the true story behind the myth of the Greek god Cupid and the mortal princess Psyche.

Cover Character Illustration: Denis Zilber
Cover, Map, and Interior Design: Bob Lentz
Production Specialist: Michelle Biedscheid

Image Credits:
Shutterstock: B. McQueen, Cre8tive Images, Natalia Barsukova, NY-P, osov, Pablo H Caridad, Perov Stanislav, Petrov Stanislav Eduardovich, Selena. Author photo: Phill Lehans.

Printed in the United States of America in North Mankato, Minnesota.
042013 007249R

NICE SHOT, CUPID!

BY
KATE MCMULLAN

STONE ARCH BOOKS
a capstone imprint

SOUTH PARK SCHOOL
DISTRICT 109
DEERFIELD,
ILLINOIS
34026 00250 9458

THUNDER COURT
PROPERTY MAP
N
Zeus's palace
T-Bolt's doghouse
Zephyr's gong
Aphrodite's temple
Barn
Smokehouse
Goat shed
Hog pen
UNDERWORLD · MAP CORPORATION

TABLE OF CONTENTS

PROLOGUE

Yep, it's me, Hades, back again to let you in on the real story behind a Greek myth. A myth you may *think* you know — but thanks to my little brother, Zeus, you don't have the foggiest.

Zeus is always having statues of himself built on top of Mount Olympus. But the only place a statue of him *really* belongs is in the Fibbers Hall of Fame. Zeus is a sneak, a shameless liar, and a total myth-o-maniac (old Greek speak for "big fat liar"). So when he got his hands on *The Big Fat Book of Greek Myths,* is it any surprise that he had all of the stories rewritten to make himself look good?

But Zeus wasn't satisfied with beefing up his own image. No, he fiddled with the myths until all his children seemed totally awesome, too. Now you know why almost all the big-deal heroes and heroines in the myths are Zeus's kids. Here, I'll show you what I mean. Check out this Zeused-up version of the story of Cupid, one of Zeus's hundreds of offspring. Go on, read it for yourself, right from the book:

APHRODITE WAS JEALOUS OF THE BEAUTIFUL MORTAL PSYCHE. SHE ORDERED HER SON, THE HANDSOME GOD CUPID, TO SHOOT PSYCHE WITH AN ARROW TO MAKE HER FALL IN LOVE WITH A HORRIBLE MAN. BUT WHEN HE SAW PSYCHE, CUPID WAS SO STUNNED BY HER BEAUTY THAT HE FELL IN LOVE WITH HER HIMSELF.

Here's the real scoop: when Cupid first laid eyes on Psyche, he was hardly handsome. He was an awkward, pimple-faced, greasy-haired teen-god with braces on his teeth. He thought Psyche was drop-dead gorgeous, but he didn't dare approach her. He figured that if she saw him, looking the way he did, she'd be totally grossed out.

So Cupid and Zeus cooked up a little scheme. They kidnapped Psyche and — listen, why don't I start at the beginning and tell you the whole story of Cupid and Psyche? When it comes to myths, you can count on me, Hades, to give you the real deal.

Chapter 1

Yo, Cupid!

I remember the day I first tuned in to Cupid's problems. I was on my way to Thebes to catch a match at Wrestle Dome, the world's newest, biggest, and most up-to-date wrestling arena. It had stadium seating, goblet holders, a sound-and-light system — the works. I could almost hear the announcer calling, "Hey, fans! Let's get ready to rumble with 'Stinger' the Giant Scorpion going up against 'Eagle-Eye' Cyclops!" What a match it was going to be! I was a huge Cyclops fan, and I had bet a bundle that he'd come out on top.

I'd just driven my chariot up from the Underworld and ridden out through my secret shortcut cave into a sunny day on earth. I turned my steeds, Harley and Davidson, onto the road to Thebes. I hadn't gone far when, off to my right, I spotted Apollo running after a young wood nymph.

"Daphne!" he called. "It is I, Apollo, god of light! Stop, and hear how much I love you!"

But Daphne ran faster than ever into the woods.

Strange, I thought. Apollo was so good-looking that goddesses usually chased after *him*.

I drove on. Before long I saw a curly-haired young man sitting by the side of the road. He was playing a sweet tune on his lyre. A dark-eyed young shepherdess stood in a nearby meadow, listening as she tended her sheep.

When he finished, the shepherdess called, "Play it again, Orpheus!"

"With pleasure, Eurydice!" the young man said. And he did.

Down the road, I passed a man with a crown on his head. He stood before a statue of a lovely woman. "Galatea!" he cried. "It is I, Pygmalion! I love you! Please, say you love me, too!"

The statue, of course, said nothing.

A few dekamiles further, I drove by a spreading tree. A pair of squirrels sat close together on a branch, chittering happily.

I wondered if they, like every other creature I'd seen so far, were chattering words of love. Curious, I tuned my godly brain to CCC — short for Creature Communication Channel — and listened in. (I was careful about how I used this godly power. I'd *never* use CCC to tune in on Cerberus, or on Harley and Davidson, or any of my own animals. You never know what you might find out that you'd rather not know.)

One squirrel was saying, *You have such a big, bushy-wushy tail.*

Oh, do you like it, Nutley? the other squirrel replied.

I clicked off my CCC and drove on. Love, it seemed, was in the air this day.

Before long, I saw Thebes in the distance. I smiled. Soon I'd be sitting in Wrestle Dome next to my buddy, King Otis, ruler of Thebes. We'd be comparing Eagle-Eye's latest stats. The Cyclops was due for a big win — and today could be his lucky day!

Suddenly, something darted across the road. I quickly pulled back on the reins. Harley and Davidson skidded to a stop, engulfing me in a brown cloud of road dust. What in the world —?

As the dust settled, I saw I'd nearly run over Cupid, the little god of love.

"Yo, Hades!" Cupid said. "Am I ever glad to see you, man!"

I hadn't seen Cupid in a couple hundred years, not since the big trial where he'd testified about zinging me with one of his arrows to make me fall in love with Persephone. (Actually, Persephone had hired him to do it — but that's another story.) I wasn't all that thrilled to see him again. I didn't trust him. The little god was a troublemaker. He got his kicks by zinging love arrows at unsuspecting mortals — or gods — and causing all kinds of confusion.

Then it hit me. No wonder everyone I'd passed on the road had been head over heels in love. Cupid was having target practice!

"Yo, Cupid," I called back to him, wondering what, exactly, *yo* meant.

As Cupid came closer, and I got a good look at him, I winced. He was going through a *really* bad teen-god stage. His hair was oily, and his face was all broken out with pimples. Even his little wings drooped like those of a molting pigeon.

"Hades, I need directions, man. How do I get to Babylon?"

"You're a god," I said. "Why not chant the astro-traveling spell?"

One big plus of being a god is astro-traveling. We think about where we want to go, chant a little spell, and — *ZIP!* — we're there.

Cupid leaned against a tree, looking dejected. "I tried that. I totally chanted the right *ZIP!* code for Babylon, but I ended up someplace called Bayonne." He rolled his eyes. "My astro-traveling powers are all messed up."

I gave him directions. Maybe he wasn't my favorite god, but I felt sorry for him. His teen troubles were so bad, they'd overwhelmed his astro-traveling system!

"Why do you want to go to Babylon, anyway?" I asked.

"I have to do some stupid errand for my mom." Cupid frowned. "Don't even get me started on her, man! She is so into looks. She makes me sick!"

"Hmmm. Well, I've got to get to Thebes," I told Cupid. "Good luck!" I picked up my reins and was about to gallop off when I realized that Cupid was still talking to me.

"First she makes me get braces. See?" He grinned. I could hardly see his teeth for all the metal. "Every time I eat, ambrosia gets stuck in them. It's really gross, man!"

But Cupid wasn't finished. "At night Mom makes me smear this bright green pimple cream all over my face. It's disgusting. And it stings. She's torturing me, man!"

Cupid went on and on. I didn't want to be rude, but I knew if I didn't get to Thebes soon, I could forget about seeing Cyclops pin Scorpion to the mat.

"She just wants me to look good so I won't

embarrass her," Cupid was whining. "She's, like, totally bummed that she, goddess of beauty, has an ugly son."

"You won't look like this forever," I said. "It's just a stage."

"Oh, right," said Cupid. "My own mom can't stand the sight of me, so she sends me off to zing mortals all over the world." He pulled a crumpled piece of parchment from his robe pocket. "In Babylon, I'm supposed to zing this chick, This-bee? Something like that. Then I have to find this dude" — he scowled at the parchment in his hand — "Pyramids, who lives next door, and zing him, too."

"You've been zinging a few arrows around here," I observed.

Cupid smirked. "Yeah. I'm trying out a couple of new love potions. Check this." He pulled three tiny golden arrows from his quiver. One was tipped in yellow, one in orange, and one in red. "The yellow is way temporary. Only lasts, like, an hour," he said. "The orange is my trusty old three-day special. That's what I zinged you with,

Hades. And by the way, Persephone still owes me for the job."

"I'll remind her," I told him.

"But this?" Cupid held up a red-tipped arrow. "This lasts, like, *forever,* man!"

"Whoa," I said. "Listen, Cupid, do you know if there's a chariot garage around here?" If I could find a place to park, I could astro-travel to Thebes in time for the match.

Cupid didn't answer. He was staring down the road. "Hey, there's Dad!" he cried.

"Zeus? Where?" I said. Now I really had to vamoose! The last thing I wanted to do was to get stuck listening to my little brother's eternal bragging.

"There!" Cupid pointed to the King of the Universe, who was racing down the road in his thunder chariot. He had just passed a young wood nymph who was picking daisies at the edge of the woods when Cupid quickly put a little arrow into his bow. "Watch this, Hades!"

ZING!

Zeus suddenly reined in his team. He leapt

from his chariot and ran toward the daisy field calling, "Yoo-hoo! Miss? You! Wood sprite, wood nymph, whatever. Minor deity! You! Stop, I say!"

The wood nymph looked up, saw the potbellied god galumphing toward her, and took off running into the woods. Zeus chased after her yelling, "Are your ears plugged up with leaves? Halt, I command you! This is the Ruler of the Universe speaking!"

I had to smile. "Nice shot, Cupid."

"Yeah." Cupid snickered. "I never miss."

"You didn't use a red arrow, did you?" I asked.

"Nah, I always zing Dad with yellow," Cupid said. "It's more fun that way."

Just then, I heard a voice calling from somewhere just behind me.

"*Cupidino?* Are you there? I have *uno lavoro*, a job for you, *mio bambino*!"

I didn't have to turn around to know it was Aphrodite, the raven-haired goddess of love and beauty. Only Aphrodite speaks that crazy brand of broken Italian. She even called her son Cupid, which comes from the Latin word for "love," instead of using his perfectly good Greek name, Eros.

Cupid looked panic-stricken. "Mom's tracked me down. I'm outta here!" He chanted some numerals, and *ZIP!* The little god was gone — somewhere.

"*Cupidino?*" called Aphrodite. "Where are you, *mio figlio*, my son?"

I didn't stick around either. "Giddy up, steeds!" I cried. "To Thebes, on the double!"

Chapter II
Big Crush!

My speed-o-meter hit 120 d.p.h. — dekamiles per hour — as my steeds raced for Wrestle Dome. When we got there, the crowd was still pouring into the stadium. I'd made it! I turned my rig over to the valet-parking mortal and hurried into the Dome. The place was packed, but I wasn't worried about finding a seat. In honor of my competing in the very first Olympic wrestling event, the management had given me a free god-size seat in the second row.

I plopped down into my seat and turned to say hello to my friend King Otis. We were both huge Cyclops fans and had gotten to be good buddies over the years. But today a mortal girl was sitting in the king's seat. I couldn't help noticing that she was incredibly beautiful, for a mortal. All the young men in the Dome were staring at her, practically drooling.

King Otis leaned forward from four seats down. "Greetings, Lord Hades," he said. "As you see, I've filled the whole row for the match today. You remember my wife, Queen Aretha?"

"Good to see you again," I told the queen.

The queen smiled. "Hey, King of the Underworld," she said.

"These are our twins," the king continued. "Muffy wears yellow, Buffy wears blue. That's how we tell them apart. And our youngest daughter, Psyche, is next to you."

"Greetings, Lord Hades," said Muffy, Buffy, and Psyche all together.

Muffy and Buffy looked exactly alike, with big brown eyes and yellow curls. Psyche had smooth olive skin and long dark hair. She looked nothing like her sisters.

"Lord Hades," said Muffy, tossing her curls. "Psyche would like to sing a song for you."

"May she?" asked Buffy.

"If she must," I muttered. Mortals often sing songs of praise to us gods. We're used to it, but lots of times the songs go on and on, and we get a little bored.

Buffy whispered, "Go on, Psyche. Do it!"

Psyche looked up at me with a pair of lovely brown eyes and began to sing:

"A hundred bottles of beer on the wall,
A hundred bottles of beer!
If one of those bottles should happen to —"

(Yep, the song's that old!)

"Daughter!" King Otis cried in horror. "Stop!"

Psyche stopped singing. The twins cracked up, laughing and snorting.

"Psyche!" snapped Queen Aretha. "Show Lord Hades some R-E-S-P-E-C-T!"

"But Muffy and Buffy said —" Psyche stopped. She folded her arms across her chest and shot her sisters a look.

Singing a disrespectful ditty for one of the most powerful gods in the universe wasn't a smart idea. But it was clear that Muffy and Buffy had set Psyche up. I knew a thing or two about sibling rivalry and playing stupid jokes. How could I not, with a brother like Zeus?

"Apologize to Lord Hades, Psyche," King Otis said, scowling at his youngest.

"Sorry, Lord Hades," mumbled Psyche.

"That's okay, Psyche," I said. "You know, we gods sing a song like that. Ours is called, 'A Hundred Goblets of Ambrosia on the Fortification.'"

Psyche smiled, and her whole face lit up. "Will you teach it to me?" she asked. And as we waited for the wrestlers to come out, I did. For a young mortal, Psyche seemed very comfortable talking with a god. Most mortals get tongue-tied. Or hide their faces in their hands and mumble "I'm not worthy!" over and over. But Psyche seemed totally at ease.

Lights began flashing all over Wrestle Dome. "Let's get ready to rumble!" the announcer called. "Today you will see mat history in the making! In this corner is a newcomer to the

Dome. Please put your hands together for the Armored Arachnid, 'Stinger' the Giant Scorpion!"

Scorpion fans went wild, yelling and shouting, "Sting him, Stinger!"

Stinger scuttled to the center of the ring, thrashing his deadly tail. He looked slippery. It was going to be tough for the Cyclops to get a hold on him without getting jabbed by that stinger.

"And in this corner," the announcer went on, "we have our One-Eyed Wonder! Let's give a Wrestle Dome welcome to Eagle-Eye Cyclops!"

All of us Cyclops fans jumped up. All together we yelled, "Make him blink, Eagle-Eye!"

Eagle-Eye stomped to the center of the ring and waved. When his eye met mine, he raised his eyebrow in greeting. He knew his biggest fan!

Muffy and Buffy started whispering together about prince somebody. How annoying! They weren't paying any attention to what was going on in the ring. But Psyche shouted, "Go, Cyclops! Stomp Stinger!" No wonder we got along so well. She was a fan!

The opponents went to their corners. You could feel the tension in the air.

DING! The wrestlers rushed to the center of the ring. They circled each other. In the blink of an eye, Eagle-Eye grabbed Stinger's tail and flipped the arachnid belly up.

"Way to toss him, Eagle-Eye!" Psyche yelled.

What a match! It went back and forth, too close to call. Finally Eagle-Eye lunged at Stinger and put him in a leg-to-tail lock. Cyclops was about to pin the Scorpion!

Psyche jumped to her feet and started chanting: *"Pin him to the mat, Cyclops! Knock that Stinger flat, Cyclops!"*

Soon all of Eagle-Eye's fans were chanting for the Cyc. The Dome was rocking!

Suddenly Stinger yanked his tail straight up in the air — with Eagle-Eye still holding on — and began thrashing it over his head. He whipped Eagle-Eye from side to side. Then, with a flick of his giant tail, he sent the Cyclops flying into the ropes. *WHAM!* Cyclops dropped to the floor. *BAM!*

Stinger shot across the ring.

"Get up, Cyc!" yelled Psyche.

But Eagle-Eye lay there, stunned, while Stinger executed a nine-point pin, using all eight legs and his tail. Eagle-Eye couldn't move a finger. The ref counted, "I, II,III! Stinger wins!"

"You'll get him next time, Eagle-Eye!" King Otis shouted at the dazed Cyclops.

Psyche shook her head. "Bummer." She looked over at me. "But it was fun cheering with you, Hades."

"Psyche! It's *Lord* Hades!" cried her mother. "What did I tell you about R-E-S-P —?"

"It's okay, Aretha," I told the queen. "Psyche can call me Hades."

We filed out of the stadium and into the parking lot, where the king's chariot was waiting. A huge crowd of young mortal men surrounded it, all with their eyes glued to Psyche.

"See you at Cyclops's next match, Lord Hades," King Otis said, helping Queen Aretha into the chariot. "He's due for a big win."

I pulled a Wrestle Dome schedule out of my robe pocket and checked the dates. "Six weeks from today, Cyclops goes up against Python."

"Can I come to that match with you and Hades, Daddy?" said Psyche.

King Otis grinned. "Why not?" he said.

The king's chariot slowly began to roll, and the lovesick young men called after it, "Wait, Psyche! Don't go!"

Muffy and Buffy looked miffed. It couldn't have been easy being the older sisters of a young mortal as gorgeous as Psyche. But Psyche didn't even seem to notice all the attention.

"Psyche, you have such nasty suitors," said Muffy, tossing her curls out of her eyes.

"Which one are you going to marry?" said Buffy, twisting a curl around her finger.

"I'm not getting married," said Psyche.

"Oooh! What was that bump?" asked Muffy. "Did we run over one of the suitors?"

"Father!" cried Psyche. "Stop the chariot!"

"Gotcha!" said Buffy. The twins cracked up laughing.

I shook my head. It couldn't have been easy being Psyche, either.

CHAPTER III
HEARTBREAKER

During the next six weeks, everything that could go wrong in the Underworld did. The worst was when King Minos misjudged some wicked ghosts. Instead of sending them to the flames of Tartarus, he sent them to the Asphodel Fields, where they went on a major crime spree.

I managed only two quick visits to my queen, Persephone, up on earth, where she was busy bringing in the spring. But I never got to Wrestle Dome. As Cyclops's match drew near, I knew I wasn't going to make it. Luckily, my cable package included the Wrestling Channel. (We gods have had high-tech gizmos for centuries — way before you mortals ever invented them.)

And so, the night of the big match, I was

sitting on the couch in the den of my palace, Villa Pluto, having a pizza. My dog, Cerberus, sat hopefully at my feet.

"Here, dog, dog, dog!" I slipped my tri-headed pooch a bit of crust. Three bits, actually.

"Hey, Hades!" Tisi, one of the Furies, came into the den. "Mind if I wait with you while Meg and Alec finish dressing?" She folded her glossy black wings and sat down beside me on the couch. "So, what are you up to tonight?"

"There's a big match on the Wrestling Channel," I said. "Eagle-Eye against Python."

"Python. He's the big snake, right?" asked Tisi.

"Right." I clicked on the TV set.

Tisi's head snakes began wiggling eagerly toward the screen. Naturally, they were all Python fans.

"Sounds exciting." Tisi picked up the Underworld newspaper, *The Hot Times*. She opened it to Page VI, which always had gossipy tidbits about doings in the upper regions. The cheesy tabloid is published by ghosts who live in my kingdom. Today's headline ran:

UNDERWORLD GOD AWOL AGAIN

It was the usual drivel about how I was spending too much time up on earth, visiting Persephone, instead of tending to my kingdom. Ghosts love to whine and complain. But I never let them bother me.

"Listen to this!" said Tisi. "Aphrodite is going to be ticked off." She began reading aloud.

"Who's the new heartbreaker in town? All the princes in the land are begging for her hand. All the mortal young women are trying to look exactly like her. Hey, Aphrodite! Is the goddess of love and beauty feeling left out these days? Are you wondering why crowds of lovesick mortals aren't packing your temples? Or why the burnt offerings aren't smoking in your direction? It's because everyone who worships beauty has abandoned you to worship at this mortal's feet. All we'll tell is that she's a young princess herself — and her name is Psyche."

"Psyche?" I yelled so loudly that Cerberus dove under the couch. "Did you say *Psyche*?"

"Yes." Tisi stared at me with her bright red eyes. "Why? Do you know this mortal?"

I nodded. "Psyche *is* gorgeous. Lots of mortal guys follow her around. But I had no idea they were deserting Aphrodite's temples!"

Tisi put the paper down. "If Aphrodite gets wind of this, I don't know what she'll do!"

"This is bad," I muttered.

Aphrodite is one of the Twelve Power Olympians. Mortals have always flocked to her temples with offerings of smoked ham, smoked oysters, smoked cheese — smoked just-about-anything — because Aphrodite is always willing to help them in their quests for love, no matter how hopeless or insane.

But Aphrodite has a bad temper. And when she gets angry — look out! She'll send out her son, Cupid, with a pack of arrows and detailed instructions. When the arrows stop zinging, you could find yourself madly in love with a cow. Or a chicken. Or a rock. She has a golden girdle (old speak for "belt"), and any god or mortal who looks at her when she's wearing it falls instantly in love with her. Then she can make them do whatever she asks. I couldn't think of a worse goddess to anger.

Meg and Alec strolled into the den. Like Tisi, they wore slim, black leather pants and black leather jackets with roomy wing slits. Each jacket had a loop-like holster where the Furies carried their scourges, the little whips they use to punish the wicked.

"Looking good, ladies," I managed. But I couldn't stop thinking about Psyche. If Aphrodite found out why mortals were deserting her temples, Psyche could be in real danger.

Tisi popped up from the couch. "Avenging calls, Hades," she said. "See you tomorrow."

I waved as they headed out into the night. Then I settled back in my La-Z-God recliner and stared at the TV screen. But as the Wrestle Dome lights began to flash, I turned off the set. I couldn't kick back and watch wrestling now. It made my ichor — what we gods have flowing through our veins instead of blood — run cold to think what Aphrodite might do to Psyche. I had to go up to Thebes and warn King Otis about possible trouble from the goddess of L&B.

I made a quick stop by my bedroom to pick up my Helmet of Darkness — a gift from my Cyclopes uncles. If things get dicey, I can put it on and — *POOF!* — I and anything I'm holding vanish into thin air. I put the helmet into my magical K.H.R.O.T.U. wallet and watched as it stretched to hold the helmet, then shrank back to its original size. I put the wallet into my robe pocket and called my dog. "Come on, Cerbie! Our chariot awaits!"

My fearless guard dog shot out from under the couch. There is nothing that dog loves more than going for a ride.

The Underworld Highway is the only way into or out of the Underworld. My kingdom is one of the few places in the universe we gods can't get to or from by astro-traveling. Even me. Luckily, I knew a shortcut. But that day, because of a major rock slide on the highway, my usual two-hour trip took six. Dawn's rosy fingers were creeping into the sky by the time I reached Phaeton's Garage, outside of Athens. I'd been planning to park there and astro-travel to King Otis's palace in Thebes. But now the garage was closed. It wouldn't open for another two hours.

"Oh, Tartarus!" (that's old Greek speak for %#!@) I exclaimed. Astro-traveling was out of the question now. What would I do with my horses? And driving to Thebes was a two-hour trip.

Suddenly, Cerberus started growling. "GRRRR! GRRRR! GRRRR!"

"Cerbie!" I said. "What is it boy, boy, boy?"

Cerberus gave a triple-snarl and ran off barking at two figures coming down the road.

"Hey, Hades!" one of the figures said as he got closer. "Call off your mutt!"

I squinted. "Cupid?"

No wonder Cerbie was barking his heads off. He'd hated Cupid ever since the little god had zinged me with one of his arrows.

"That dog of yours is a menace!" Cupid said.

"Cerbie, cease!" I commanded.

Two of his mouths snapped shut, but the third still bared its teeth at Cupid.

I found the can of Cheese Yummies I keep in my chariot for emergencies and threw a handful into the backseat. Cerbie stopped growling and leaped over the seat to get them.

"Go sit on a log or something, Grub," Cupid said to his traveling companion, a mortal.

Grub nodded, scratched his belly, and trotted off obediently to find a log. I'd never seen anyone more disgusting. Greasy hair hung halfway down his face, stubble dotted his chin, and out from under his filthy robe poked two thick and hairy legs. What was the god of love doing with such a repulsive mortal?

"What luck bumping into you, Hades," said Cupid. "Can I ask you a favor?"

"Make it fast," I told him. "I'm in a hurry."

"Okay. Can I borrow your chariot?"

"My chariot? You must be joking!"

"I'm not," said Cupid. "See, Mom sent me out to find the grossest, smelliest, most disgusting mortal in the world."

I glanced over at Grub. He was sitting on a log with a finger up his nose. "Looks as if you found him," I said.

"Yeah." Cupid nodded. "Found him in Sparta, cleaning out a goat pen."

That explained the smell.

"Now I'm supposed to zing this mortal chick," Cupid went on, "and make her fall in love with Grub. Mom said to use a red arrow, make it last forever."

"A cruel fate." I made the mistake of looking at Grub again. He'd taken off his sandals and was picking things from between his toes. "Who is this unfortunate mortal woman?"

Cupid dug in his pocket and pulled out a scrap of parchment. "Her name's Psycho."

"Let me see that!" I grabbed the parchment. "It's not 'Psycho'! It's *Psyche*!"

"Whatever," said Cupid.

So Aphrodite had heard the news. And this was her way of getting revenge on her rival — by making her fall in love with Grub!

"You can't do it, Cupid," I told him. "Psyche is a lovely young princess. She has only one short little mortal life to live. She deserves better than to spend it with a smelly slob like Grub!"

"She'll be in love with him, man." Cupid smirked. "She won't mind."

"If you have to zing her," I said, "at least find her a nice guy. There are hundreds of suitors following her around. Pick one of them."

Cupid shrugged. "Mom won't give me my allowance if I don't do what she says."

"So don't tell her!" I practically yelled.

"She'll find out, man," Cupid said. "She always does."

This I could believe.

"Anyway, Mom said Psycho lives in a palace near Thebes," Cupid went on. "She told me to find her *pronto* — and when Mom says *pronto*, she means, like, yesterday. She'll be all over me if I don't get this done. Astro-traveling is a nightmare for me these days, so I really need your chariot, Hades."

I made a fast decision. "All right, Cupid, you can use my chariot."

"Hades!" Cupid exclaimed. "You are the dude, man!"

I nodded. This solved my parking problem.

Now I could astro-travel to King Otis's palace and warn him that Cupid was coming. By the time the god of love showed up with Grub, Psyche would be long gone.

I whisked Cerbie out of the backseat of the chariot. "It's all yours, Cupid. Drive carefully, obey the speed limit, and when you're finished, bring it back here, and park it at Phaeton's."

"Cool, Hades," said Cupid. Then he yelled, "Come on, Grub! We got wheels."

Grub shuffled over. "Nice wagon," he grunted.

Harley flared his nostrils and gave me such a look. Davidson whinnied unhappily. I patted my steeds. "Oh, come on, he doesn't smell *that* bad," I whispered.

But as he passed me to climb into the chariot, I realized he did.

"Let's go, stallions!" Cupid said, and my steeds galloped off toward Thebes.

Then, holding on to Cerbie, I chanted a little ditty and traveled to Thebes the godly way: *ZIP!*

Chapter IV

Head Over Heels

I landed outside of King Otis's palace, a big white marble affair set on a hilltop overlooking Thebes. From where I stood, I could see the big round roof of Wrestle Dome.

"Stay, Cerbie." I put him down and gave him a pat, pat, pat.

I hurried toward the palace, passing dozens of suitors waiting for a glimpse of Psyche. I saw that King Otis had hired a couple of big burly bouncers to keep them in line. I went straight up to the front door and knocked. After a long time it opened. There stood Muffy and Buffy.

"Is your father home?" I asked.

Muffy shook her head. "He and Mom went to Crete for a little vacation."

"Where's Psyche?" I asked.

"Up in her tree house," said Muffy.

"Singing songs to birdies," said Buffy. She made a circle in the air by the side of her head, indicating that her sister was a little nuts.

"I've come to warn Psyche of danger." And I told them about Aphrodite's cruel plan.

"Psyche's going to fall in love with the smelliest man in the world?" said Muffy.

"Forever?" said Buffy.

And the sisters burst out laughing.

"It's no laughing matter!" I said. "Cupid will be here soon. Psyche must go into hiding."

But Muffy and Buffy kept laughing. They obviously thought it would be a great joke if their gorgeous little sister ended up married to a smelly slob. I sighed. I'd have to save Psyche from Grub myself.

"Tell Psyche to pack an overnight bag and come out here on the double," I said.

Muffy and Buffy nodded. Then, still laughing, they shut the door.

I paced back and forth in front of the palace,

thinking. Maybe there was an unused dressing room in Wrestle Dome where I could hide Psyche.

I kept pacing. What was taking Psyche so long? Maybe she was like my Persephone. Packing always took her forever. And so I paced some more. Finally, I couldn't take it any longer. I pounded on the palace door.

No one answered.

"Muffy! Buffy!" I yelled.

Finally, Muffy came to the door.

"Where's Psyche?" I asked her.

"Buffy and I are helping her get ready to meet her new suitor," she said, giggling. "We want her to look her best."

"Just tell her to hurry!" I said.

A ruckus over in the suitor's line caught my attention. Cerbie started growling. I turned — and there were Cupid and Grub! Cupid must have driven my steeds at full gallop all the way. Now I had to move fast, or Psyche would be stuck with Grub forever!

I yanked my helmet from my wallet, and as soon as it grew back to its full size, I clamped it onto my head. *POOF!* I disappeared. I whisked Cerbie up and put him down behind a tree.

"Cerbie, stay!" I said again. "I'll call you if I need you to sink your teeth into Cupid."

Cerbie wagged his stumpy tail.

Meanwhile, Cupid was trying to convince the bouncers that he was a god, so they couldn't keep him out of the palace yard. At last he succeeded and began steering my chariot up the walk. He stopped at the entrance, hopped out of the chariot, and yanked Grub out too. Positioning the dirty mortal in front of the palace door, he said, "Stand right here, and don't *move*!"

If Psyche opened the door now, the first thing she'd see would be the smelly mortal.

Cupid ran over to the side of the palace and hid in a clump of bushes. He removed a tiny red-tipped arrow from his quiver. "Yo, Psycho!" he called.

I ground my teeth. Why couldn't he get her name right?

"Psycho!" he called again. "Come out here!"

I inched invisibly toward Cupid, getting ready

to tackle him the second the door cracked open. But it remained shut.

Cupid yelled, "Come, Psycho! True love awaits you!" He raised his bow.

The palace door opened. Cupid put the arrow onto his bowstring and pulled it back. He closed one eye, taking aim.

Psyche appeared in the doorway. She had on makeup — lots of it. Obviously, Muffy and Buffy had been working on her. She looked around, blinking in the sunlight. She saw Grub, and her black-rimmed eyes widened in surprise. "Who are you?" she asked.

The time to act had come. I ran forward and lunged at Cupid — it was a great move, a lunge worthy of Eagle-Eye. I was inches from pouncing on the little god when he suddenly ducked behind a tree. *OOF!* I hit the ground, flat on my belly. It was an awkward moment, and I was glad no one could see me. I scrambled invisibly to my feet, ready to tackle him again. But when I saw Cupid, I stopped mid-move.

The little god stood still as a statue, staring at

Psyche with his mouth open. His bow slid from his hands and dropped in front of him. I smiled. There was only one explanation for this sudden change in behavior. The god of love had just fallen head-over-heels in love.

Grub stood still as a statue too, obeying Cupid's orders not to move.

Muffy and Buffy were hanging out of two upper-story windows of the palace. Psyche turned and looked up at them. "What's going on?" she asked. "Who is he?"

"Grub," called Muffy. "Your new suitor."

"Go get her, Grub!" called Buffy.

Grub's beady eyes lit up. He shuffled toward Psyche, his arms open wide.

"Come to Grub!" he called. "You love Grub!"

"I've never even seen you before!" said Psyche.

"Kiss him, Psyche!" called Muffy.

"Go on!" said Buffy.

"Yes!" cried Grub. "Kiss Grub!"

"Oh, right!" Psyche laughed and started singing.

"Won't kiss Grub, and I don't care!"

Won't kiss Grub, and I don't care!

Won't kiss Grub, and I don't care!

And now I'm gone away!"

She turned and ran back into the palace, shutting the door behind her.

"Come baaaaaack!" Grub bleated. "Come baaaaack!"

With Psyche out of sight, Cupid came to his senses. "Oh, man!" I heard him murmur. "Psyche is so beautiful. No wonder Mom is worried."

Cupid ran out from behind the tree. "Let's go," he said to Grub. He grabbed the confused, smelly mortal by the elbow and began dragging him toward the chariot.

"Wait!" wailed Grub. "Wait for Psycho!"

"No!" said Cupid. "This whole Psyche deal is so over!"

I smiled as I watched Cupid toss Grub into my chariot and gallop away from the palace. Cupid was much too in love with Psyche himself to zing her and make her fall in love with Grub now — or with anyone else.

"Let's go, Cerbie," I said, picking up my pooch.

"Row-rooooo!" wailed Cerbie. He was clearly disappointed that I hadn't called him to sic Cupid.

"Next time, Cerbie," I told him. "Let's go home. Aphrodite's little scheme just fizzled. Psyche is safe now. Cupid won't bother her again."

That's what I thought then.

But I couldn't have been more wrong.

CHAPTER V

HERE COMES THE BRIDE

"Go, Eagle-Eye!" I shouted. "Score on the Boar!"

I'd made it up to Wrestle Dome at last. I'd been dying to see the Cyclops in action for months now, ever since I'd missed watching him wrestle Python. (The snake had squeezed a victory out of that match.)

Here came Eagle-Eye now, making his way down the aisle. The crowd cheered.

"Go, Cyc!" I yelled.

Tonight Eagle-Eye was wrestling the Calydonian Boar. He was a tough opponent, but I was sure this was going to be Eagle-Eye's big comeback.

I glanced at the seat next to mine. Still empty.

That was strange. I didn't get up to Wrestle Dome very often, but King Otis hardly ever missed a match. Where was the king tonight?

Now Boar trotted down the aisle. He was a hairy one. His huge curved tusks ended in sharp points. He raised his forehooves over his head, grunting loudly to the thrill of his fans. The match was about to begin. I leaned forward in my seat.

DING! Eagle-Eye and Boar began circling each other, keeping to the outside of the ring.

Suddenly King Otis rushed down the aisle.

"Hey, Otis," I said, taking my eyes off the Cyclops. "You made it."

"Oh, Lord Hades!" cried the king. "A terrible thing has happened. I need your help again!"

"Of course," I said, watching the circling wrestlers. "Sit down, and tell me the problem."

"AYYYY-YA!" Flames shot from the Boar's snout as he did his famous flying-hoof thrust. Eagle-Eye ducked. Then he hit Boar with his shoulder, knocking him to the mat. *THUD!* All right!

"Please!" said the king. "Come with me now!"

"Uh, now?" Eagle-Eye had Boar on his back. The fans were going wild.

"Now!" he said. "I beg of you!"

I sighed and got up. "Go, Eagle-Eye!" I yelled at my champ. "Start makin' bacon!" Then I followed King Otis up the stairs and out of Wrestle Dome. I couldn't believe I was going to miss his match — again.

I squeezed my godly form into the passenger seat of the king's chariot, and we galloped off, heading north out of Thebes. King Otis was as big a Cyclops fan as I was — maybe bigger — so I knew something must be terribly wrong, or he'd never have asked me to leave the match.

"Thank you, Lord Hades," said King Otis once we were out of the city. "You see, three nights ago, I was awakened by a voice. It shouted, 'King Otis! Go at once to the oracle at Belphi!'"

"Don't you mean Delphi?" I asked.

"That's exactly what I asked," said King Otis. "But whoever it was shouted, 'No! Belphi! It is just south of Thebes.'"

"An oracle south of Thebes?" I said. "Never heard of it."

Mortals — and gods, too — often used to go to oracles to ask sibyl priestesses what the future held in store. Would they marry? Would they have children? Who should they put their money on in the big chariot race? But this was the first time I'd ever heard of a mortal being awakened in the night and ordered to go to an oracle. Very strange. "Could you tell who was speaking?"

The king shook his head. "It was a very commanding voice, so I felt I must obey. I set out immediately, and just south of Thebes, I saw a sign with an arrow. It read **BELPHI, THIS WAY**. Soon I came to another sign. It read **BELPHI, STRAIGHT AHEAD**. I followed the signs to the mouth of a cave."

King Otis paused as he steered his horses to the right, up a steep hill.

"I stepped into the cave," the king went on. "There sat a sibyl. She had on a veil, so I never saw her face. But she told me the most awful news!" He brushed away a tear. "She said that a terrible six-winged serpent had seen my Psyche and fallen in love with her."

"What?" I cried.

The king nodded. "She said that my lovely daughter was fated to marry this serpent!"

"Oh, cruel fate!" I cried.

"The sibyl said that the following night, I was to take Psyche to the top of Craggy Peak," the king continued. "The very peak we are climbing now. She said I was to leave Psyche there all alone, and in the dead of night, the serpent would come to claim his bride."

Poor Psyche! First she almost got zinged into falling in love with the world's smelliest mortal. And now she had to marry a serpent? It didn't seem fair. Had Aphrodite dreamed up this new scheme after the failure of her Grub plot?

The hill got steeper and steeper. "I begged and pleaded with the sibyl," the king said. "I offered her riches. I offered my kingdom. I offered myself as a servant to the serpent. But the sibyl said Psyche must be brought to Craggy Peak that very night, or she would perish."

"And what did Psyche say when you told her?" I asked.

"Psyche was very brave," the king said. "She went straight to her room and packed. She never shed a tear. She said, 'Father, if it is my fate to marry a serpent, so be it.'" The king shook his head. "Her mother and I broke into sobs. So did Muffy and Buffy — although I later found out they were crying because they thought it was so embarrassing to have their sister married to a serpent."

At last, we reached the top of Craggy Peak. The king reined in his horses. We got out of the chariot and walked to the edge of a steep cliff. "I brought Psyche here last night to wait for the serpent, Orp."

"Wait a minute," I said. "I know Orp. It can't be Orp!"

"No?" said the king, brightening slightly.

"Not a chance," I told him. "Orp has been sleeping peacefully down in the Underworld for centuries. The last time I saw him was at my wedding. My lieutenant, Hypnos, woke him up so he could attend the ceremony. At the reception, I remember Orp pretty much devoured one whole buffet, table and all. But when the dancing started, he crept back to his lair."

"He . . . he doesn't sound dangerous," the king said.

"Orp is big, but he wouldn't hurt a flea," I said. "Orp didn't take Psyche."

"But the oracle said —" the king began.

I cut him off. "That oracle is as bogus as the fake blood pouring from a head wound at a wrestling match, Otis. There is no Belphi. Sibyls don't wear veils. And Orp never carried off your daughter!"

The king looked puzzled. "But, Lord Hades," he said, "I brought Psyche here last night, to this very spot. And now she is gone. If Orp did not carry her off, then who did?"

"I don't know — yet," I said. "But don't worry, Otis. I'll get to work on it right away. By this time tomorrow, I'll have some answers for you."

The king thanked me and headed back down the hill. I quickly astro-traveled back to Wrestle

Dome, hoping to make it in time to catch the tail end of the match. But I was too late. When I arrived, crowds were pouring out the doors.

"Did Eagle-Eye beat the Boar?" I asked a passing mortal.

"Nah," the mortal said. "The Cyclops got stomped."

"Oh, Tartarus!" I grumbled. If only I'd been there to cheer him on, he might have won.

CHAPTER VI

SERPENT IN LOVE?

It was late by the time I got back to Villa Pluto. I went straight to the Furies' wing. "Tisi!" I called. "Meg! Alec! Are you there?"

"We're here!" Tisi called back. "Getting ready to go out!"

"Before you go, come see me in the den. We have an emergency!"

I walked into the den. Cerbie was there, curled up on the couch between Hypnos, the god of sleep, and his brother, Thanatos, god of death. None of them woke when I came in.

I grabbed a Necta-Cola, sat down in my La-Z-God, and shifted into recline. Ah, now I could think. But the more I thought about Otis's story, the less sense it made. All I knew was that someone had carried out an elaborate plan to spirit Psyche away. Aphrodite was the number-one suspect. But somehow this crazy plot didn't sound like the way she'd operate.

Before I could think of who else might be responsible, the Furies burst into the room.

"We're here!" said Tisi. Like her sisters, she wore a shiny black hooded slicker and shiny black boots. They must have heard it was raining on earth.

"What's going on?" asked Meg.

"Tell us *now*!" said Alec.

"It's Psyche," I said, bringing my chair back to an upright position. "Remember that Page VI item from *The Hot Times*, Tisi?"

"About mortals deserting Aphrodite's temples to worship Psyche's beauty?" asked Tisi.

I nodded. "Now someone's kidnapped Psyche." And I told them the strange tale Psyche's father had told me.

"A phony oracle?" said Tisi. "A fake sibyl?"

"And accusing poor Orp!" said Meg

"*Nasty!*" said Alec. "Who's behind this?"

I shrugged. "That's what I'd like you Furies to find out."

"We have a full schedule of avenging tonight, Hades," said Tisi. Her sisters nodded.

"Psyche's mother is beside herself with sorrow," I added, knowing this would make the Furies fighting mad. Their main job is punishing mortals who have offended their mothers.

Meg bared her fangs. "We'll ask around," she said. "We'll find whoever kidnapped Psyche."

"We'll make them *sorry*!" said Alec, fingering her scourge.

"That's the spirit, my winged avengers!" I said. Then, with Cerbie at my heels, I walked with them out into the palace yard. There, the Furies spread their mighty wings and rose into the air. "Good luck!" I called after them as they flew away.

When they were out of sight, I put my thumb and first finger in my mouth and gave a series of long, loud whistles.

"Owww! Owww! Owww!" Cerbie howled.

"Shh, Cerbie!" I said. "This is my Orp call. He won't be able to hear it if you're yowling."

Cerbie sat down and pretended to sniff a nearby clump of asphodel.

I whistled again. And a third time.

At last I heard a faint whirring. The noise grew louder. Soon, the big bulbous shape of Orp flapped into view. He flew low, hardly higher than my head. His six thin, lacy wings were pitifully small for the size of his body — he was a very stout serpent — and flying was difficult for him. But he made a smooth landing just this side of the Pool of Memory, folded his wings, and slithered over to me. When he reached me, he yawned, and I saw all six rows of his teeth, plus his tonsils.

At our wedding reception, Cerbie had discovered that Orp was a sloppy eater. He'd followed the serpent around, licking up the crumbs. Now he ran in circles around Orp, happily yip-yip-yipping.

Orp coiled up his rear half, gave his head a wake-up shake, and in a breathy voice said, "You whisssstled, Lord Hadesss?"

"I did, Orp," I replied. "There is a rumor

going around on earth that you have taken a wife."

"Me?" Orp's half-lidded pink eyes stretched wide. "Take a sssspouse?"

I nodded. "There is a king in Thebes who says you are in love with his daughter, Psyche. That you have swooped down and stolen her away."

"Sssswooped? Sssstolen?" Orp seemed truly puzzled.

"I didn't think so," I told him.

"I lead a ssssolitarty life, Lord Hadessss," Orp said. "I wissssh I had a ssssweetheart. Ssssomeone to share my dreamsss with would be niccce." Orp sighed. "Maybe if I had a sssweetie, I wouldn't sssleep sssso much. Or have put on ssso many poundsss."

"Why do you think whoever kidnapped Psyche put the blame on you, Orp?" I asked.

"Oh, that'ssss easssy," said Orp. "In my younger, sssslimmer dayssss, I wass a wild and crazzzzy sssserpent. I sssspirited off a number of sssprites, nymphsss, naiadssss, and sssuch. No mortalsss, though. But I sssuppose it'ssss possssible that my dangerousss reputation sssstill ssstands."

Orp seemed pleased by the idea that it might.

"Anything elssse, Lord Hadessss?" asked Orp.

"No, Orp," I said. "I just wanted to hear it directly from you that you had nothing to do with Psyche's disappearance."

"I'm innocccent," said Orp. "Well, sssince I'm up, I might assss well ssscoot up to earth and ssssearch for sssome breakfassst." Orp's little wings popped up from his back. Then, with much wheezing and flapping, the serpent lifted off and flew away.

"Ooooowwww!" Cerbie howled after him. I could tell the pooch was disappointed. Orp hadn't dropped a single crumb.

I rose early the next morning. I wanted to meet the Furies when they came home. I was eager to find out if they'd learned anything about Psyche. But they had no news. Night after night, I sent them out on the same mission: find Psyche. But morning after morning, they came back with nothing.

Time passed. Persephone came home to Villa Pluto for the winter, and before long I took her back to earth to bring another spring. I'd nearly given up hope of finding Psyche. Then one morning, while I was sipping my nectar java, the Furies came to see me.

"We've found Psyche," Tisi announced.

"Is she all right?" I asked.

"She's fine," said Meg.

"But she's *lonely*!" said Alec.

"Where is she?" I asked.

Tisi handed me a carton of blueberries she'd brought from earth. "Make us a batch of your ambrosia-blueberry pancakes, and we'll tell you everything."

How could I refuse?

Once the Furies were sitting down, digging into my pancakes, Tisi began the story. "You told us that Psyche was last seen on top of Craggy Peak. We have gone there many times. We have tried flying from the cliff to see where we ended up."

"We flapped our wings as hard as we could," said Meg.

"But it was always too *windy*," said Alec. "We went *nowhere*."

"Last night we went to Craggy Peak again," Tisi said. "We stood at the edge of the cliff. It was very windy. But this time, as we unfurled our wings, the West Wind, Zephyr, spoke to us. She said that no being, no matter how powerful, could take off from Craggy Peak without her help."

"Why is that?" I asked, putting a second round of pancakes on Tisi's plate.

"We asked her the same thing," said Tisi. "She said there was some sort of a barrier there. No one can fly or astro-travel from that peak."

"Odd," I said.

"We asked Zephyr if she had helped someone fly Psyche from Craggy Peak," said Meg.

"And she said she had carried Psyche from Craggy Peak *herself*," said Alec.

"Aha!" I saw that Meg had finished her first stack. The Furies always worked up a hearty appetite avenging. I poured more batter into my skillet. "Where did she take Psyche?"

"To Thunder Court," said Tisi.

"Thunder Court?" I frowned. "Is that some gathering place of the storm winds?"

"No," said Meg. "It's Zeus's palace in the far, far northwest corner of the world."

"Zeus!" I cried. "I should have known he was up to his neck in this mess. That phony oracle had Zeus's fingerprints all over it. And the Craggy Peak barrier? That is pure Zeus!"

"Calm down, Hades," said Meg.

"Let us *finish*!" said Alec.

"Sorry," I muttered as I flipped the pancakes. "Go on."

"Zephyr blew us to Thunder Court," said Tisi. "She complained the whole time."

"She feels unappreciated," said Meg.

"*Unloved!*" said Alec.

"She set us down at Zeus's palace," said Tisi. "It's fantastic. All the walls are pink marble. All the columns are gold with silver trim. It has a grand courtyard and —"

"I don't care about the palace. What about Psyche?" I cut in.

Tisi shot me a red-eyed glare. She always likes to give a sense of place for her stories.

Meg picked up where her sister had left off. "We walked toward the palace," she said. "Zeus's vicious guard dog barked at us and snarled."

"Luckily, she was *chained,*" said Alec.

"Very lucky." I took Meg's plate and gave her a refill. "But did you find Psyche?"

"We *did*!" said Alec, holding out her empty plate. "Psyche lives all alone in the palace except for a staff of invisible nymphs who wait on her and bring her meals."

"Zephyr told us that these nymphs used to work for Zeus and Hera up on Mount Olympus," said Tisi. "One time they saw Zeus flirting with a minor goddess, and they told Hera."

"Hera let it slip to Zeus that the nymphs had caught him being unfaithful," said Meg.

"It made Zeus *mad*!" said Alec.

"To punish the nymphs, he made them invisible, so he would never have to look at them again," said Tisi.

"And then, to make it worse, he took away

their voices, so they could never tattle on him again," said Meg.

"Then he had Zephyr blow them to Thunder Court to be his *servants,*" said Alec.

"Poor nymphs," I said, turning over Alec's pancakes. "But what about Psyche?"

"She can stroll freely in the palace and the gardens," said Tisi.

"But a high wall around the courtyard keeps her inside," said Meg.

"She's a *prisoner*!" said Alec.

"This just doesn't sound like Zeus somehow," I said. I handed Alec her seconds. "What's his motive? There must be more to it."

"We didn't have enough time to learn more," said Tisi.

"Zephyr came back," said Meg. "She was about to blow back to Greece for the night."

"She said, 'If you want a ride home, let's go *now*!'" said Alec. "So that's all we know."

"Congratulations on a job well done, Furies." I poured the last of the batter into the skillet. This next batch was mine. "I think I'll go to the top of Craggy Peak and ask Zephyr to blow me to Thunder Court. I'll pay Psyche a visit myself."

"Let us know what you find out," said Tisi.

"Tell us everything," said Meg. "Oh, and Hades? Good pancakes."

"*Excellent!*" said Alec.

Chapter VII

Love Speaks

After I finished my pancakes, I put my helmet in my wallet. I tossed in a shaker of Ambro-Salt, too. It's one way we gods can make sure we have a daily dose of ambrosia, the food of the gods, when on the road. Then I drove up to earth and astro-traveled to Craggy Peak. I stood on the edge of the cliff. I wasn't sure how winds liked to be summoned, so I tried a few different approaches. "Hello, Zephyr? Come in, Zephyr! Do you read me, Zephyr?"

I'd already tried astro-traveling to Thunder Court, but I'd gone nowhere. "Yoo-hoo, Zephyr!" I called.

Two puffs of warm wind hit my face. "I'm here, I'm here. Don't get your pants in a bundle," said a raspy voice.

"Zephyr? Is that you?" I said. "It's Hades here, King of the Underworld. Remember me?"

"Of course," the West Wind said. "I'm just surprised you remember who I am. Oh, everyone knows my brothers. Boreas, the North Wind, blows freezing winds that make mortals' teeth chatter. Notus, the South Wind, blows tornados. They can wipe out entire cities! And me, the West Wind? I blow a warm, gentle breeze. Good for flying kites. Wind surfing. You'd think gods and mortals would appreciate old Zephyr. But do they? Noooo."

"Don't be silly," I said. "The Furies told me you blew them to Thunder Court. *They* appreciate you."

"Ah, I was useful to them. That's all. I'm used to being used."

"The Furies said it was a great ride," I told Zephyr. "They enjoyed getting to know you."

"Really?" said Zephyr.

"No kidding," I told her. "You think you could take me there too?"

"I get it," said Zephyr. "You want to use me too. Well, why not? Everyone else does."

As she spoke, Zephyr blew a gust so strong that I found myself suddenly airborne.

"I have a feeling Zeus wouldn't like you going to Thunder Court," Zephyr said, propelling me through the air. "And that's reason enough for me to take you. Even the big shot Ruler of the Universe doesn't get to have his way all the time."

Zephyr wafted me over mountains and oceans. She gave a smooth ride. As we went, I listened to her endless whoosh of words.

"Zeus has so many secrets," Zephyr said. "And I have no one to tell secrets to. That's why he picked me to blow everyone to Thunder Court. Without me, no one can get there. I blew over all the workers who built his monstrous pink palace. I blew over all the silver, gold, and marble, too. Marble! Never again! That stuff weighs a dekaton! And did Zeus thank me? Three guesses."

"You can tell me his secrets," I said. "Why did Zeus have you take Psyche to Thunder Court?"

"Why indeed," said Zephyr. "You know, Thunder Court used to be a jumping joint. In his marrying days, it was Zeus's favorite honeymoon spot. That's why he put in the big heart-shaped bathtub. Zeus and Aphrodite lived there for a while right after they were married. But now Zeus only ducks in to hide when Hera's caught him flirting with a mortal or some wood nymph. He keeps me going back and forth, though. Like a shuttle service! No errand too small for ol' Zephyr."

"Um-hum," I said. She hadn't exactly answered my question. "Sounds like Zeus."

I heard thunder rumbling in the distance. Zephyr gusted me lower and lower. "We are making our final approach for landing," she said. "Our flying time today was I hour and XLIX minutes. The temperature on the ground is LX degrees. Set your sundials for 11 p.m. TCT — Thunder Court Time."

I peered down at a huge compound of pink buildings. Zeus always has to make the grand statement, even out here in the middle of nowhere. The pink palace itself was titanic, ten times the size of Villa Pluto. Around it were dozens of smaller pink buildings and deka-acres of beautiful flower gardens, all surrounded by a high stone wall. Outside the wall, I could just make out specks I thought must be sheep, grazing beside a river.

Zephyr set me gently on the ground just inside the wall.

"I suppose you'll need a ride back," she said.

I nodded. "How do I reach you?"

"See that gong?" asked Zephyr, pointing to a big gold disk hanging beside the gate. "One *bong*! That's all it takes to summon me. All right, I'm gone."

"Thanks for the ride, Zephyr," I told her.

Zephyr swirled around me, making a little tornado in the dust. Then she breezed off.

I didn't want to be seen at Zeus's palace, so I shook my Helmet of Darkness out of my wallet, put it on — *POOF!* — and began walking invisibly along the garden paths toward the palace. I passed pink marble servants' cottages, a pink marble carpenter's shed, a pink marble smokehouse, a pink marble laundry hut, and an amphitheater with pink marble benches. I passed a pink marble temple dedicated to Zeus and one decorated with pink marble doves in honor of Aphrodite. I passed a pink marble barn, a pink marble chicken coop, a pink marble hog pen, and a pink marble goat shed. I sniffed. Whew! Zeus's goats smelled nasty.

Just then I saw a pink marble doghouse with **T-BOLT** chiseled over the door. As I passed, T-Bolt thrust her head out and snarled. She was black-and-tan with pointy ears, fierce coal-black eyes, and a mouth full of sharp white teeth.

"Nice doggie," I said.

Crouching low and still growling, T-Bolt slunk out of her doggie palace. I was invisible, but with her keen sense of smell, she knew exactly where I was. Today she wasn't chained.

"Chill, T-Bolt." Luckily, the Furies had warned me about Zeus's dog, and I was prepared. I pulled a fistful of Cerbie's Cheese Yummies from my robe pocket and tossed one into the air.

"Treats, T-Bolt," I said.

The treat appeared in midair, and the dog caught it.

By the time I'd tossed a few Yummies, T-Bolt

was wagging her tail. She let me walk on, unmolested, toward the palace. I smiled. So much for Zeus's watchdog. Cerbie would *never* let anyone enter the Underworld for a few measly Cheese Yummies.

Just as I was about to go into the palace, Psyche came out the door. She looked slightly older than the last time I'd seen her. But being kidnapped and held prisoner had not spoiled her looks. In fact, I thought, she was lovelier than ever — for a mortal.

Humming to herself, Psyche skipped down the steps and made her way to a reflecting pool beside a marble temple. I followed invisibly behind her. She sat down on the grass and stared into the pool. I was amused to hear her start singing "A Hundred Goblets of Ambrosia on the Fortification" to herself in her sweet, high voice.

Aphrodite's temple hid the little pool from view of the palace, so I decided it was safe for me to take off my helmet. "Psyche?" I said softly.

Psyche looked up eagerly. "Voice?" she said. "Is that you?"

What was Psyche talking about? "It's me, Hades," I said.

"Hades!" exclaimed Psyche. "But where are you?"

"I'm wearing a helmet that makes me invisible," I said. "I'll take it off now."

FOOP!

"Wow!" Psyche said as I appeared. "Cool trick. Did my father send you?"

I nodded. "He asked me to find you," I said. "It took a while."

"Oh, how are my father and mother and sisters?" asked Psyche.

I sat down across from her in the grass. "They're fine. Worried about you, of course."

"You're the first person — I mean, god — I mean, anybody! — I've seen in a whole year. Well, sometimes I talk to the goatherd, but he doesn't have much to say. The servants around here are invisible, and they never say a word. The only way I know they're around is when I see lunch floating toward me. It's very strange. But I'm used to it now."

"Do you know who this palace belongs to, Psyche?" I asked.

"To Voice, I guess."

"Who's that?"

"I'm not sure." Psyche shrugged. "Late at night, when I'm in my room in the palace, Voice speaks to me from behind a velvet curtain. We talk for hours."

"What sort of a voice is it?" I asked.

Psyche thought for a moment. "A nice voice. It tells me funny stories and makes me laugh. When I talk to Voice, I'm never lonely."

"And you've never looked behind the curtain to see who the voice belongs to?"

"I want to!" Psyche said. "But Voice made me promise not to look. He said if I did, he could never come to see me again. And if I didn't have Voice to talk to, I'd go nuts."

"Who do you think it is?" I asked her.

"At first, I figured it was Orp," Psyche said. "I thought I'd freak if I saw him. But nothing Voice said made it sound like he was a serpent, so one night I said, 'You're not a serpent are you,

Voice?' And Voice said, 'No.' So then I begged to look behind the curtain, but Voice always said the same thing: 'No way, José.'"

"Very mysterious." I wondered if Voice could be Zeus. But hiding behind a curtain wasn't at all his style.

"I'll take you home," I said. "I'll call Zephyr."

Psyche frowned. "I miss my parents and my sisters," she said. "But if I left here, I'd miss Voice even more. We talk about everything — how our families drive us crazy, what music groups we like, what games we like to play. Voice is so funny. He knows a million jokes! And I play songs for him on my harmonica. I've never had a friend before. Back home, Muffy and Buffy were so close. But I was lonely. Hey! I know! Could I bring Voice home with me?"

"That depends on who Voice is. I'll go see what I can find out." I stood up.

"Wait, Hades," said Psyche. "Can't you hang around for a while? I'd love the company! And hey, how's old 'Eagle-Eye' Cyclops doing, anyhow? Has he won any matches?"

"Not lately," I told her. "He needs you there to cheer him on."

Psyche grinned and started chanting, "Pin him to the mat, Cyclops! Knock that Stinger flat, Cyclops!"

I smiled too. "I'll let your father know you're all right. But do me a favor. Don't tell anyone — even Voice — that I was here. I'll be back soon."

"Make it *really* soon, okay, Hades?" said Psyche. "I thought I was fine, spending the days all by myself, but you know what? Now that I've seen you and talked to you, I realize I'm pretty starved for company."

"I hear you." I raised my helmet and put it on my head. *POOF!*

"Bye, Hades," said Psyche. "Wherever you are."

"I'll be back," I told her. "And remember, not a word about me being here."

"Okay!"

I made my way to a secluded spot in the rose garden, where I sat down, pulled out my phone, and gave Persephone a call.

"Phoney, honey?" I said when she answered. "It's me, Hades. I've found Psyche."

"Hades! That's great. Wow, there's so much static on the line. Where are you?"

"At Thunder Court, Zeus's secret palace hideaway," I said. "Could you take a message to King Otis for me? Let him know that Psyche is fine."

"Glad to do it, Hades," said Persephone.

"So, how's spring going?" I asked.

"The ants are eating up my strawberries this year, Hades," she said. "I plant them, and all I get is a bunch of anthills and half-eaten berries. I've had it! I'm not planting any more strawberries. Blueberries, blackberries, gooseberries, okay. But no more strawberries."

"You're making me hungry, P-phone." It had been a while since those blueberry pancakes. "I think I'll go raid Zeus's refrigerator."

After we hung up, I made my invisible way into Zeus's kitchen. No invisible servants stopped me from opening his fridge and helping myself to some very tasty ambrosia-stuffed grape leaves and a bottle of Necta-Cola. Stuffed myself, I went upstairs to have a look around. I peeked into several empty bedrooms before I found Psyche's. An oil lamp stood on the bedside table beside piles of books and games. A harmonica lay on the bed. And at the far end of the room was a thick black velvet curtain. Aha!

I walked over and pulled the curtain aside. Whoa! Psyche's side of the room wasn't exactly neat, but this half looked as if Eurus had been here, blowing a tornado! Random sandals littered the floor. Wet towels had been thrown over the backs of chairs. A couch was piled high with dirty robes. I picked one up. It was small — Zeus could never have crammed his tubby body into it. I picked up a sandal. Not so small, just old and scuffed. But still no clue to the identity of Voice.

I yawned. It was hours until Psyche's bedtime, hours until Voice began to speak. I decided to catch a few z's. There were plenty of empty bedrooms. I'd set my mental alarm clock for X o'clock, then tiptoe invisibly back here and get a look at Voice.

I pulled the black velvet curtain back, just the way it had been, and went out of the door in the messy half of the room. I made my way to the empty bedroom next door, where I crawled invisibly into bed. After what seemed like only minutes, I awoke to the sound of Psyche laughing. I ran out into the hallway and put my ear against the door.

Voice was speaking. "And I swam all the way back to Greece," it said.

"You are so making that up!" said Psyche.

"Am not!" said Voice.

"Well, if you can do that," Psyche said, "you can bring my sisters here to visit me."

"No way!" said Voice. "I'll bring anybody you say to visit you. Anybody except your sisters."

"I don't know anybody but Muffy and Buffy," said Psyche. "Come on, Voice. My sisters will be totally awed when they see your cool palace."

"No! Don't ask that, Psyche! Come on. You know they'll just cause trouble."

"Please, please!" begged Psyche. "I'm by myself all day long. I need somebody to talk to, or pretty soon I'm going to start talking to myself. Bring my sisters. Come on!"

"It'll be a disaster, man!" said Voice.

Wait a minute. I knew that voice!

"Then *you* come see me in the daytime, Voice," Psyche said. "I'd rather be with you than anyone."

"I can't," said Voice. "Not yet. Hey, I know! I'll get you a puppy!"

"I don't want a puppy!" said Psyche. "A puppy can't talk. I want my sisters!"

The voice groaned. "Aw, man!"

But — it couldn't be! Slowly, carefully, I turned the doorknob. Slowly, carefully, I pushed open the door and peeked into the candlelit chamber. And at last I laid eyes on the mysterious Voice.

It was none other than the little god of love himself, Cupid!

Chapter VIII

Love Busted!

What was Cupid up to? Once Psyche went to sleep, I'd get him to tell me what was going on. I leaned invisibly against the wall to wait.

Cupid wadded up a couple of his dirty robes for a pillow and stretched out on the couch. "Sing me a song, Psyche."

He looked a lot happier than the last couple of times I'd seen him.

"Trying to change the subject, Voice?" Psyche said. "It won't work." She began to sing:

"Say you'll bring my sisters here,
Charming Voice! Charming Voice!
Say you'll bring my sisters here, charming Voice!"

Then Psyche lowered her voice, as if answering for Voice.

"Yes, I'll bring your sisters, dear,
They can stay for one whole year!
For you're a young thing, and you must have your sisters!"

Cupid couldn't help but laugh at Psyche's silly song. "All right. You win," he said. "I'll send word to your sisters to go to Craggy Peak tomorrow morning. Zephyr can pick them up and bring them to visit you. But no way are they staying for a year!"

"That would be too long," agreed Psyche. "But I needed a rhyme."

"Why am I doing this?" Cupid muttered. "It's a terrible idea!"

"It isn't!" said Psyche. "But will you still come talk to me? Even if my sisters are here?"

"I'll think about it," said Cupid. "Night, Psyche."

"Good night, Voice," said Psyche. "And thank

you!" The light faded from under the curtain as she put out her lamp for the night.

Cupid hopped up and began throwing his robes and sandals into a little gym bag. I waited a few minutes to give Psyche time to fall asleep. Then I whispered, "*Psst!* Cupid!"

Cupid jumped. He looked around. "Who's there?" he whispered. "Who said that?"

I took off my helmet and — *FOOP!* — appeared before him.

Cupid gasped. "Hades! What are you doing here? You're freakin' me out, man!"

"And you freaked out a lot of mortals when you kidnapped Psyche," I told him. "What's going on, Cupid?"

Cupid folded his scrawny arms across his chest. "None of your beeswax, man!"

"Psyche's father is a friend of mine," I said. "He begged me to find out what happened to his daughter." I threw a wet towel off one of his chairs and sat down. "So talk. Now!"

"Zephyr's coming for me, Hades!" Cupid said. "I can't keep her waiting."

"Then talk fast."

"Oh, all right," Cupid said. "But not here. We'll wake Psyche." He quickly finished stuffing his robes into his gym bag and zipped it shut. "Come on."

I followed Cupid down the stairs to the palace dining room. We sat down across from each other at Zeus's long gold dining table.

"Okay, Hades, here goes," said Cupid. "Remember when Mom ordered me to zing Psyche and make her fall in love with Grub?"

I nodded.

"I took Grub to the palace where Psyche lived, set him up in front of the door, and called her to come outside. I was all ready to zing her. Then she came to the door, and I got my first look at her, and I'm like, WOW! Come on, Hades. You've seen her. She's totally, unbelievably beautiful! It was like love at first sight, man!"

"Why didn't you zing her with an arrow and make her fall in love with you?" I asked.

"What fun would that be, man?" said Cupid. "Sure, she'd love me. But I'd always know it was only the potion."

I could relate. When Cupid had zinged *me*

all those centuries ago, I didn't know whether I loved Persephone for real or only because of his arrow. It was very confusing.

"Go on," I told Cupid. "What did you do then?"

"Psyche went back into the palace," said Cupid, "and I yanked Grub away from the door — no way was I going to make her fall in love with *him*! I was going to take Grub back to the goat shed where I'd found him, but Sparta is so far away, man. And all I could think about was how I could get Psyche to fall in love with me for real. I knew that if she saw me all pimply and geeky, she'd be, like, 'Get me out of here!' So I was really mixed up about what to do. Then it hit me. The perfect god to help me figure it all out — Dad!"

I groaned. "You went to Zeus for advice?"

Cupid nodded. "I turned my chariot around — oops! I mean *your* chariot, Hades — and I drove over to Mount Parnassus."

"No wonder Harley and Davidson were so beat when I picked them up from the garage,"

I muttered. "But why did you go to Mount Parnassus?"

"Dad and Apollo are thinking of buying the oracle at Delphi," said Cupid. "You know, as an investment property. I knew they were there, checking it out. I found Dad and told him how I'd fallen in love with Psyche, but how I was afraid she wouldn't like me because of the pimples and being a major brace-face and stuff, and Dad came up with a genius plan."

"I'll bet."

"First, he got Psyche's dad to go to this oracle."

"So Zeus was the voice in the night that commanded King Otis to go to Belphi?" I said. "The *fake* oracle?"

"Right!" said Cupid. "We totally fooled that old mortal. We put up signs pointing to this empty cave. And you know my half sister, Thalia, the muse of comedy? She's always ready to play a good joke, so Dad talked her into pretending to be a sibyl. She wore a veil over her face, and when King Otis showed up, she told him that a serpent had fallen in love with his daughter."

"That would be Orp?" I said.

"Yeah, well Orp was a mistake." Cupid shrugged. "Thalia said she just blurted out that it was a six-winged serpent, and then she started going on and on about him, and when she had to come up with a name, the only one she could think of was Orp. But we all figured it was cool, since no one has seen Orp for centuries, because he's asleep down in the Underworld."

"Not anymore," I said. "Go on."

"So the next night, King Otis brought Psyche to the top of Craggy Peak," said Cupid. "And when her dad left, Zephyr picked her up and flew her to Thunder Court. Dad says I can keep her here as long as I want."

"But if you love her, how can you keep her a prisoner?"

"It won't be for long," said Cupid. "Just until I get better looking."

"What?" I cried.

"Yeah, you know, when my skin clears up,

and my hair isn't so oily, and I get my braces off, and I work out and get some muscles, then I'll let Psyche see me," said Cupid. "Then I'll be really good looking, so she'll love me back!"

I jumped out of my chair. "That is the *worst* plan I've ever heard!"

"Huh?" said Cupid. "No, man! It'll work!"

"For starters, Psyche is a mortal," I said. "Mortals have short life spans. By the time you get your braces off, Psyche will be an old woman. Or maybe even a ghost down in my kingdom."

"It won't be *that* long, Hades!" Cupid cried. "Every night I totally cover my face with the pimple cream Mom gave me. It's working — no kidding! Check out my chin. Only one little zit! And Mom says I can get my braces off in a couple of years."

I rolled my eyes. "Cupid, just show yourself to Psyche. Trust her to see beyond the metal on your teeth and a few red bumps on your face."

"No way, José! Mom's always told me that love and beauty go together," he said. "You can't have one without the other. That's why she's goddess of them both."

"But she didn't mean —" I began.

"Zephyr's waiting." Cupid jumped up and grabbed his gym bag. "I've got stuff to do! I promised Psyche I'd bring Muffy and Buffy here. And I've got to get home. If I don't get there every three or four days, Mom starts tracking me down. I know she suspects something. She's always asking me a million questions. Once I even caught her following me! If she ever finds out that I love Psyche, she'll freak out, man! 'Cause, you know, Mom totally hates her guts!"

I nodded. "I know."

"Plus," said Cupid, "I've got to bring in some mortal food for Grub."

"Grub?" I said. "He's here?"

"Yeah. The nymphs won't go near him."

"But why?" I asked.

"'Cause he stinks, man," said Cupid.

"No, I mean why is he here at Thunder Court?"

Cupid sat back down. "See, when I got to

Mount Parnassus, I told Grub to get lost. But he kept wailing about how he didn't know how to get home. And he kept wailing about 'Psycho.' Smelly mortals, man. You give 'em a dekainch, and they want a dekamile." Cupid shook his head. "Grub started dogging me, Hades. Everywhere I went, he'd show up. I couldn't lose the guy! And when I went up to Craggy Peak to get Zephyr to blow me to Thunder Court, he showed up."

"He wanted to be with Psyche?"

Cupid nodded. "Zephyr was totally into bringing him here. She thought it would be a great joke on Zeus to have a smelly mortal hanging around his palace. He lives in the goat shed."

That explained the awful smell.

"Since the palace nymphs won't feed Grub," Cupid went on, "I have to pay Zephyr to bring food in for him. It's a nightmare!"

"Sounds like it."

"Okay, I'm gone," said Cupid. "And Hades? Don't tell Psyche that I'm Voice. Promise?"

In spite of myself, I felt sorry for Cupid. It wasn't easy being a teen-god. I sighed. "Promise."

"Thanks, Hades!" And with that, the little god of love ran out of the palace to catch the wind.

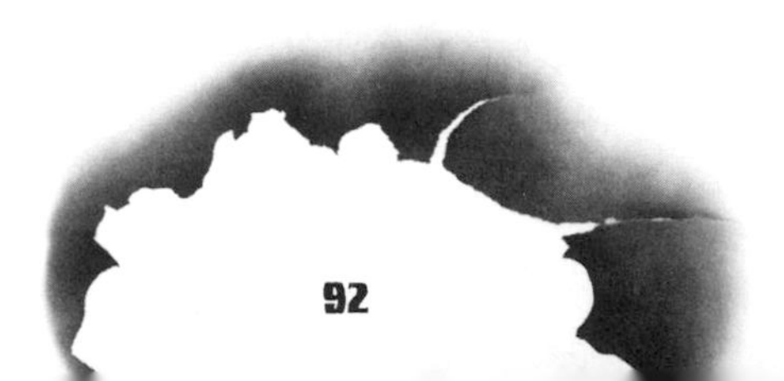

Chapter IX
Sister Love

I called Persephone the next day.

"Are you still at Thunder Court, Hades?" she asked. "We've got a terrible connection."

"I'm still here," I said. "I spent the night in an empty bedroom, and I way overslept." I told her all that I'd learned the night before.

"Poor Cupid!" said Persephone. "His mom is so obsessed with beauty that she's made him feel awful about his looks. Doesn't he know that most teen-gods go through an awkward stage?"

"You didn't, did you, P-phone?"

"I was a mess, Hades," said Persephone. "Tall and scrawny and always tripping over my own feet. You must have gone through it too."

"Who knows?" I said. "I grew up down in

my dad's belly, remember? There weren't any mirrors."

"Anyway," said Persephone, "it's terrible that Cupid feels so bad about himself. Can't you help him, Hades?"

"I'm doing my best, P-phone. Listen, I have to get some nectar java. Then I'll try to see if I can't get Psyche out of here and take her home."

"Bye, Hades," said Persephone. "Good luck!"

"Bye, Phoney!" I put on my helmet — *POOF!* — and headed down to the kitchen. I was too late for java. I'd even missed lunch. All I could find was a Necta-Cola and a stale roll. I strolled invisibly out to the palace courtyard. I thought I'd eat my roll in the rose garden. But when I reached the courtyard, I heard mortals yakking.

"This is the serpent's palace?" one said.

"Psyche lives here?" said another.

Had to be Muffy and Buffy.

"Don't apologize." This from Zephyr. "Just because you kept me waiting all morning. And don't thank me, just because I blew for hours to get you here."

"You won't get any thanks from us," said Muffy.

"That was the bumpiest ride ever!" said Buffy.

I gulped my Necta-Cola, stuffed down the roll, and hurried toward the voices. I caught sight of the sisters walking toward the palace. They had bags slung over their shoulders. Maybe Muffy and Buffy could talk Psyche into going home.

Psyche ran out of the palace to greet her sisters. "Muffy! Buffy!" she cried, throwing her arms around them. "You both look great!"

"As always," said Muffy, tossing her curls. "Have you heard? I'm engaged to Prince Ducius."

"I'm engaged too," said Buffy. "To Prince Geus."

"You can have a double wedding!" said Psyche. She hummed a few bars of "Here Comes the Bride."

"We'll live in palaces, too," said Muffy. "Only bigger than this one."

"So, Psych, where's the serpent?" said Buffy.

"Um, I don't know," Psyche said. "He usually stops by at night."

"He's probably too ugly to be seen in broad daylight," said Muffy. "So give us a tour of the palace."

Psyche led them inside. Of course, I stuck invisibly with them. "This is the living room," Psyche said.

"So small," said Muffy.

"Horribly cramped," said Buffy.

"Do you like the fountain?" asked Psyche, gesturing toward a golden basin with twelve life-sized silver dolphins spewing water out of their mouths. "We can go for a swim in it later."

"My prince and I are going to have a fountain like that," said Muffy. "Only ours will have *gold* dolphins."

"My prince and I will too," said Buffy. "Only ours will have gold dolphins *and* whales."

"This is the dining room," said Psyche. "The table seats one hundred."

"That's all?" said Muffy.

"How can you possibly throw a dinner party?" said Buffy.

"My bedroom is up here," said Psyche, leading

her sisters up the stairs. She opened the door to her room. "Isn't it nice? I have so many books and games. Hey, I learned to play the harmonica." She picked it up. "Listen!"

"Not now," said Muffy.

"Or ever," said Buffy. "What's behind that musty old curtain, anyway?"

"I — I don't know," said Psyche. "Each night Voice speaks to me from behind it. But I gave my word never to try to see him."

"Orp must be totally gruesome, or he'd let you see him," said Muffy.

"Does he smell bad?" asked Buffy.

"No!" said Psyche. "In fact, I don't think he's a serpent at all."

"One way to find out," said Muffy. "Let's take a look behind the curtain."

"No!" said Psyche. "Um — how would you like to see the jewel cabinet?"

"Jewels?" said Muffy.

"Where?" said Buffy.

Psyche led her sisters down the hall to a big cabinet where Zeus displayed the biggest example of each kind of gemstone in the world. Muffy and Buffy stared longingly at the gems, including grapefruit-size diamonds and turnip-size rubies.

"You think Orp would mind if we took a couple of the emeralds?" said Muffy.

"They're so little," said Buffy. "He'd never miss them."

"I can ask him," said Psyche. "Hey, you must be hungry after your long trip — I'll call the servants. They'll bring us dinner."

"How many servants do you have?" asked Muffy as the sisters made their way back downstairs.

"I'm not sure," said Psyche. "They're all invisible."

"Doesn't that give you the creeps?" said Buffy.

The table had been set for three while the sisters toured the upstairs. "It used to," said Psyche as they sat down. "But I'm used to it now. I just wish they'd talk to me once in a while," she added as she rang a small golden bell.

Soon, platters of food began to float in. The

invisible nymphs brought the sisters soups and salads and skewers of shish kebab. It all looked delicious! I wondered whether they'd notice if one of the skewers floated up into the air and disappeared. Hmm. Too risky.

Muffy and Buffy started shoveling in their dinners.

After three helpings, Muffy wiped her mouth with the back of her hand. "It wasn't very good," she said. "I could hardly choke it down."

"It was awful," Buffy said with her mouth full. "And such small portions."

"So tell me everything that's happening back home," said Psyche as the dirty dishes floated off the table. "How are Mom and Dad?"

"Fine," said Muffy. Then she and Buffy told Psyche all about their wonderful, handsome husbands-to-be. They told of dancing all night at the clubs in Thebes. They talked on and on.

Poor Psyche. She sat there looking more and more miserable. What was there to say about a mysterious Voice?

"How about some dessert?" Psyche said at

last, and she rang her little golden bell. Almost instantly, platters of melon, peaches, grapes, and figs floated in. "Cookies would be good with this. I'll go see if we have any." She got up from the table and hurried off to the kitchen. I knew she wasn't looking for any cookies. The poor mortal needed a few minutes of peace!

I was about to go after her when Muffy and Buffy started talking. When I heard what they were saying, I stayed right where I was.

"Psyche must have hundreds of servants," said Muffy. "Way more than I'll ever have!"

"She lives in such luxury!" said Buffy, winding one of her ringlets into a knot. "She's totally spoiled, just like she was back home. Mom and Dad always loved her better than us. And now she gets all *this*." She spread her hands wide, indicating the marble, the gold, the silver. "She's the youngest. It isn't fair!"

"Not fair at all," said Muffy. "Okay, so she has to live with a serpent. Big deal. I'd rather be married to a snake any day than to Prince Ducius. He is such a clod."

"I know," said Buffy. "Prince Geus is a moron."

"Plus, can you believe how good Psyche looks?" said Muffy. "She's gorgeous. And there isn't even anybody around to look at her. She makes me sick."

"Me, too," said Buffy. "No wonder we hate her."

"Let's play a dirty trick on her," said Muffy. "The way we used to."

Buffy smiled.

I couldn't believe it. Psyche's sisters were eaten up with jealousy!

Psyche came back to the table, looking a little strained. "The cookies will be right out."

Muffy took a slice of melon. "We enjoy being with our fiancés so much," she said. "It's a pity you never get to see Orp."

Psyche only nodded.

"Or maybe it isn't, since he's a disgusting monster," said Buffy.

"Actually," said Psyche, "he doesn't sound disgusting at all."

"I see he has lulled you into trusting him," said Muffy, flicking her curls out of her eyes.

"That's a terrible mistake," said Buffy, winding her hair around her finger.

Psyche frowned. "You think so?"

"Oh yes!" said Muffy. "A terrible mistake."

Suddenly, my stomach growled.

"What was that?" said Buffy, looking around.

"Oh, probably one of the servants," said Psyche.

Oh, Tartarus! There it went again.

"Something's growling," said Muffy.

"Maybe Orp is home," said Buffy. "Does he growl, Psyche?"

My empty stomach would just keep growling unless I fed it, so I tiptoed out to the kitchen, where I found an untouched shish kebab. Yum! Zeus is not my favorite brother, but he sure had some excellent cooking nymphs at Thunder Court. I took all the leftovers out of the fridge, sprinkled on some Ambro-Salt, and ate my fill. Feeling much better, I hurried back to the dining room.

Muffy and Buffy had their heads together, whispering. Psyche was nowhere to be seen. I leaned closer to hear what the terrible twins were saying.

"She promised," said Muffy. "Psyche always keeps her promises."

Buffy giggled. "It's just like the old days. She'll do whatever we tell her to!"

What were they talking about? What promise?

"Do you think the serpent will harm her?" said Muffy.

"Who cares?" said Muffy. "Her flirting got her into this fix. She can get herself out of it."

I didn't like what I was hearing, so I headed for the stairs to check on Psyche. I was halfway up the stairs when an ichor-curdling scream pierced the air.

CHAPTER X

BURNING LOVE

I raced up the stairs three at a time as another horrible scream rang out. I burst into Psyche's room. It was empty. The screams were coming from behind the curtain. I ran over and yanked back the heavy velvet folds. Psyche knelt on the floor, sobbing. Beside her, an oil lamp lay on its side. The screams seemed to be coming from the mouth of a small green-faced monster. But — it wasn't a monster. It was Cupid!

His face was smeared with the thick green pimple cream, and he was wearing red pajamas dotted with little pink hearts.

"WAAAAAAH!" wailed the god of love.

"I'm so sorry!" Tears streamed down Psyche's face. "Let me bandage your wound!"

"No! Stay away!" Cupid held a sheet to his shoulder. "You've hurt me enough already!"

"I only wanted to see your face!" cried Psyche. "I never meant to spill hot oil on you."

"Well, you did! You burned me!" Cupid cried. "And I never wanted you to see me with pimple cream all over my face!"

"Is that what it is?" Psyche said. "Pimple cream?"

"Yes!" shouted Cupid. "I've got pimples, okay? Oh, why couldn't you have trusted me?"

"I wish I had!" cried Psyche. "I never should have listened to my sisters!"

I turned and saw Muffy and Buffy peering around the door frame on the far side of the room. They snickered as they watched the scene before them.

"I wasn't ready to show myself to you yet," Cupid whined. "I can't believe you snuck in and caught me like . . . like this! With goo on my face and braces and greasy hair!"

"I don't care about those things!" cried Psyche.

"Well, I do!" yelled Cupid. "I wish I'd zinged you and made you fall in love with Grub, the smelliest mortal in the world! Then you'd know what suffering is!"

"I do know!" cried Psyche. "I'm suffering right now!" She reached out to Cupid. "Let me see how bad your burn is, Cupid. Let me help you!"

"No!" cried Cupid, drawing back. "The only one who knows how to help me is my mom! I'm going home to her right now!"

Suddenly, someone spoke up behind me. "No need to, *bambino mio*! I, your *madre*, have come to you!"

I looked over my shoulder, and was I ever glad I was invisible! I gave three silent cheers for my Helmet of Darkness.

Aphrodite, goddess of love and beauty, tossed back her raven curls. Then, opening her arms wide, she teetered toward her green-faced son on a pair of ridiculously high-heeled sandals.

"Mom!" cried Cupid. He flew into her arms.

"Yech!" Aphrodite exclaimed. "Oh, *caro mio*, your pimple cream! All over my new robe!" She wiped a small tear from one of her gorgeous sea-blue eyes.

I wondered if she was weeping from joy at seeing her son or because he'd ruined her robe.

Cupid drew back from his mother. "Mom, how did you know I was here?"

"I knew you kept secrets from me, *mio cattivo ragazzo*, my naughty boy!" said Aphrodite. "Always flitting off. Only coming back to *La Casa* when you had a *grande* bag of dirty laundry. So I followed you. *Si!* So strong is my love for you that I followed you to the far corner of the earth!" She beamed at her son and pulled him close. But when she spoke again, her voice had lost its sweetness. "But where do I find you, *Cupidino*? At Thunder Court, Zeus's secret hideaway. With *her*!" She thrust a finger at Psyche.

Psyche swallowed. "I'm sorry I hurt Cupid," she managed. "I never meant to!"

"Careless mortal!" Aphrodite stared at Psyche for a moment. Then she said, "I heard you were *si bella*, so beautiful. But no, I don't see it. Your chin, it is weak. Your eyes, they are so small and close together. Your hair, it is a disaster. Oh, how could those foolish mortals abandon my temples for the likes of you? Their eyesight, it must have failed them. Why, I have ten times your beauty. Twenty times —"

"Mom!" cried Cupid. "Stop talking! Look at my wound!" He pulled back his pajama top and pointed to where the hot oil had splashed onto his shoulder.

It was a minor wound, not worth much fuss. But I knew what really pained Cupid was that Psyche had seen him with his green-creamed face and braces.

"Oh, *mio bambino!*" crooned Aphrodite. "*Caro mio!*" She hugged Cupid to her already green-stained robe and shook a fist at Psyche. "*Imbecille!* How could you hurt *mio figlio*, my son?"

Cupid whimpered, "Make it stop hurting, Mom!"

I thought Cupid's whining might make Psyche think she was better off without him. But the poor girl fell to the floor. "I am sorry, Cupid!" she cried. "So, so sorry! Please, forgive me!"

Aphrodite picked up her gawky son and held him in her arms. *"Andiamo, Cupidino,"* she said. "Let's go." With one high heel-sandaled foot, she shoved Psyche's limp form out of the way and tottered off down the palace hallway.

Psyche groaned and threw herself onto Cupid's couch. She sobbed as if her heart would break. "Oh, why did I ever beg for my sisters to come here?" she wailed. "By not trusting Voice, I have lost true love!"

I stayed invisibly by Psyche as she wept. Her sisters were still peeking from the doorway. To them, the poor girl appeared to be crying her heart out all alone. Surely now, I thought, the twins would come and put their arms around Psyche to comfort her. But when I glanced back at the doorway, Muffy and Buffy weren't there.

Psyche sobbed pitifully for a long time. At last, I couldn't stand it anymore.

"Psyche?" I whispered, taking off my helmet. *FOOP!* "It's me, Hades." I patted her gently on the back. "Don't take it so hard. Cupid was upset, but he'll calm down."

"But I hurt him!" cried Psyche, crying harder

than ever. "I burned him. And I broke my promise to him."

"Worse things have happened," I said. "He can forgive you."

Psyche looked up at me with swollen, red-rimmed eyes. "I would do anything — ANYTHING! — to make that happen! Please, tell me what I can do to help Cupid forgive me."

I sat on the edge of Cupid's couch, patting Psyche on the back and thinking. The wound on Cupid's shoulder would heal. But how could she heal the wound in his heart? And even if Psyche convinced Cupid to forgive her, she still had a terrible enemy in Aphrodite.

Aphrodite — she was the key. She'd made Cupid feel bad about his looks. She was the reason Cupid had to hide his love away. "I think I have an answer for you, Psyche," I said at last.

"What, Hades?" she cried, wiping the tears from her cheeks. "Tell me!"

"You won't like it," I said.

"Please!" she begged. "I'll do whatever it takes!"

"If you want to win Cupid back," I said, "you'll have to win over his mother first."

"His . . . mother?" Psyche blinked as she tried to understand what this might mean.

"It will be incredibly difficult," I said. "Aphrodite is so jealous of your beauty that she has hardened her heart against you."

"I got that," said Psyche. "What's with the weird way she talks, anyway?"

"She's showing off," I said. "It's supposed to be Italian."

"But why?" asked Psyche.

"Long ago, when we gods first lived up on Mount Olympus, Zeus went down to Earth, fathered lots of immortal children, and sent them up to Mount Olympus," I told her. "It was a dynasty thing. When Aphrodite showed up, we all assumed she was one of Zeus's kids. Then we learned that she had really risen from the foamy sea near the island of Cythera, fully grown."

"Strange," said Psyche.

"She floated over to Cythera, then went to Italy and stayed there for a while before coming up to Mount Olympus. She's sensitive about her strange birth, so she claims to have the soul of an Italian, and she's always trying to prove it. That's why she gave her son a Roman name."

Psyche shook her head. "She's scary."

I agreed. Aphrodite could be hard to take.

"There is one thing in your favor, though," I told her. "As the goddess of love, Aphrodite must help any mortal in love who comes to ask for her assistance."

"Really?" said Psyche. "I'm a mortal in love! You mean she has to help me?"

I nodded. "But she doesn't have to make it easy."

"I'll go to her now," Psyche said. "I'll offer to be her servant, I'll learn Italian, I'll do whatever it takes to make Aphrodite change her mind about me."

"That's the spirit!" I said.

Psyche jumped up and smoothed her rumpled robes and her damp, tear-soaked hair. She turned to me. "Thank you, Hades. Wish me luck!"

"Good luck, Psyche!" I said. She walked bravely out into the palace hallway and didn't hear me add, "You'll need it."

CHAPTER XI
MAMA LOVE

I thought maybe I'd better be around when Psyche tried to talk to Aphrodite. Just in case. So I put on my helmet — *POOF!* I was on my way out of the room when I spotted Cupid's bow and his quiver full of arrows lying on the floor. In all the confusion, he must have dropped them. I put the bow and quiver into my K.H.R.O.T.U. wallet and slipped it into my pocket. Then I followed the sounds of voices down the hallway.

As I went, I heard feet running on gravel. I glanced out a window and saw two figures running across the moonlit courtyard. It was Muffy and Buffy heading for the gate, dragging their bulging bags behind them. Those bags hadn't looked like that when they arrived. Had they stolen Zeus's jewels? When they reached Zephyr's gong, Muffy picked up the mallet. *Bong!* Well, good riddance to bad sisters!

I rounded a corner and nearly bumped into Aphrodite. The goddess of L&B stood with her arms outstretched, blocking the door to a room where, I guessed, she'd put Cupid to bed.

Psyche was kneeling before her. "But I *do* love Cupid!" she said. "With all my heart. I will do anything you say in order to see him again."

"*Vai via!* Go away!" said Aphrodite. "Haven't you hurt *mio bambino* enough already?"

"Please!" begged Psyche. "I am a mortal in love. You must help me, Aphrodite, for you are the goddess of love!"

Aphrodite put her hands on her hips. "Go fall in love with a mortal. *Capisci?* Understand? Then I will help you."

"I cannot," said Psyche. And she began to sing, ever so softly, "My heart belongs to Cupid —"

Aphrodite put her hands over her ears. "*Basta!* Stop that yowling! So! In addition to your

countless other faults, you are also tone-deaf and stubborn!"

"I am steadfast in my love," said Psyche.

I had to hand it to Psyche. She was standing up to an angry goddess — not an easy thing to do.

"*Va bene,*" said Aphrodite. "All right. Here is my best offer. The only way you'll ever see *Cupidino* again is to do the tasks I give you."

Uh-oh. Tasks. This was not a good sign. As used by the gods, *tasks* can mean almost anything. Tasks are easy for gods and goddesses to think up. And a lot of the time the tasks are nearly impossible for poor mortals to carry out.

But Psyche had no idea what she was in for. "Give me tasks!" she cried. "I'll do them!"

Aphrodite smiled. "So, you are willing to work your fingers to the bone?"

"I am!" said Psyche.

"You must work *note e giorno,*" Aphrodite said. "Night and day, never stopping."

"No problem," said Psyche.

It wasn't hard to see what Aphrodite had up her sleeve. She planned to work the poor girl until she lost her beauty. Then, she thought, her *Cupidino* would fall out of love with Psyche.

"And you must make me *uno promesso*, a promise," Aphrodite went on. "That you will ask no mortal or god to help you."

"I promise," said Psyche.

"*Andiamo!*" said Aphrodite. "Let's go."

Aphrodite picked up a lantern. She led the way down the stairs and out of the palace, with Psyche at her heels. As we hurried past the pink marble doghouse, I heard T-Bolt snoring. Some watch-pup. Across the moonlit courtyard we went, following the goddess of L&B to the pink marble barn, where she threw open the doors.

"*Bene*. Good," said Aphrodite, looking down at a huge pile of grain in the middle of the barn. "It is here, as in the old days when I lived at Thunder Court." She turned to Psyche. "Do you see that stack of grain?"

"How could I miss it?" said Psyche.

"A harvest of wheat, barley, and rye," said Aphrodite. "Each kind of grain must be sorted into its own pile. Then I will take some rye and bake *il pane*, bread, for my poor *Cupidino*." Aphrodite eyed Psyche. "This is your first task."

"I can do it!" declared Psyche.

"By *domani*, tomorrow morning," said Aphrodite. "*Capisci?* Understand?"

"Tomorrow?" Psyche stared at the pile. "But it's already after midnight now!"

"Tomorrow morning," said Aphrodite. "Or you will have failed. *Ciao!* So long!"

With that, the goddess of L&B turned around and swept out of the barn, slamming the doors behind her.

Psyche could never separate all the grains in the few hours given to her. Aphrodite's task was impossible! But if I stepped in to help her, and Aphrodite caught me? Psyche would be disqualified. She'd lose Cupid forever.

Psyche stared up at the mountain of grain. "You are all that stands between me and my true love," she told it. "You are nothing I can't handle."

Brave words, but the stack just sat there, looking bigger than ever.

Psyche sat down on the dirt floor of the barn

where a bunch of ants were running around, gathering seeds. Her face lit up. "I promised not to ask any god or mortal to help me," she said. "But Aphrodite didn't say anything about ants. Come here, ants! I have a favor to ask you. A BIG favor!"

No ants came over to her, of course. They couldn't understand her. But Psyche had come up with a good idea. She hadn't asked me for help, so it wouldn't be her fault if I just gave her plan a little boost.

I squatted down and put the old brain into CCC. *Queen of ants?* I thought. *It's me, Hades. Make yourself known to me, please.*

A stream of words flowed into my head. *Queen Thorax here. What is it?*

There's a young mortal in the barn tonight. She needs the help of your worker ants.

Psyche was still calling, "Over here, ants. Who wants to play a game of Sort the Grain?"

She must separate the grains in the stack into piles of wheat, barley, and rye, I thought to the queen of the ants.

That's a big job, the queen replied. *It will cost you.*

By tomorrow morning, I added.

A rush job! We charge triple for those.

Is there anything that I, Hades, can do for you, Queen Thorax?

Actually, there is something.

Name it, I thought to her. *It's yours.*

There's a nasty rumor going around that Queen Persephone has nixed planting any more strawberries this spring. Anything you could do to change that?

I'll speak to Persephone. I'm sure she'll see it your way.

Consider the grains sorted, thought Queen Thorax.

Even before I had shifted out of CCC, thousands of ants began scurrying toward the grain pile from every direction. They lifted the grains and carried them off.

"Yes!" cried Psyche. "I knew I could count on you ants! Three piles, please. Wheat, barley, and rye. Here, I'll sing to make the work go faster."

"The ants go marching one by one, in single file.
The ants go marching one by one, in single file!
The ants go marching one by one,
To heap the rye in its own high pile,
Then they all go marching back, to the stack,
To repeat, with the wheat. Boom, boom, boom . . ."

The ants sorted the grain while Psyche sang verse after verse of her song. By the time Hyperion's son, Helios, drove his sun chariot into the eastern sky, the little workers had separated the three types of grains into three neat stacks.

Only moments later, Aphrodite swung open the barn doors.

"So! I knew you could never —" She stopped short when she saw the three piles of grain. "*Incredibile!*" she cried. "Someone helped you."

"Neither mortal nor god," said Psyche.

"No matter," said Aphrodite, calming herself. "This was *si facile*, so easy; it was hardly a task at all. Let me show you your next task. This one you won't find so simple." She snapped her fingers at Psyche. "*Andiamo!*"

CHAPTER XII

BAA-BAA LOVE

Aphrodite led the way toward the big wooden gate in the courtyard wall. At her approach, an invisible nymph threw open the gate, and Aphrodite breezed out into the meadows surrounding Thunder Court. Psyche and I followed as she hurried on to the top of a high hill. Down below was a wide river. A large flock of sheep nibbled grass in the valley beside it, their fleece glowing like gold in the early morning light.

The goddess of L&B pointed down the hill. "*Guarde!* Look!" she said. "There you see Zeus's flock of sheep. Killer sheep."

"Killer sheep?" Psyche's eyes opened wide. "I thought sheep were gentle creatures."

"Not these sheep," said Aphrodite. "Their fleece is made of *oro*, gold, and they will fight fiercely to protect it."

Leave it to Zeus to have sheep that grew Golden Fleece! I wondered who he'd stolen them from.

"I wish to have a *grande* bag full of *oro* fleece," said Aphrodite. "It must come from just one sheep — the flock's leader, *Signore* Rambow. He has the brightest fleece. I will have it woven into a golden *coperta*, cover, to put over my poor, wounded Cupid."

At the mention of Cupid's wound, Psyche shut her eyes. But when she opened them, she looked more determined than ever. "I'll get you a bag of Rambow's fleece, Aphrodite," she said.

"You may use my golden shears and my collecting bag," said the goddess of L&B, handing them to Psyche. "I must have my fleece by sundown, or you will have failed to do this task. *Capisci?*"

"I understand," said Psyche, staring down at the sheep. "By sundown."

Psyche tied the bag around her waist, stuck the golden shears into her girdle, and set off toward the sheep. The hill was steep and covered in thorny bushes. By the time she reached the sheep meadow, Psyche was scratched and bleeding.

I made my way down the hill too. I'm not proud of this, but I astro-traveled to get there. I mean, what good would come of my working up a drosis (old Greek speak for "god sweat") and getting scratched up from thorn bushes and ichoring all over the place? I needed to concentrate on helping Psyche.

When she reached the valley, Psyche began inching slowly toward the flock, calling, "Here, sheep! Nice Rambow. How about giving me some of your beautiful golden wool?"

The flock was about fifty strong. I spotted Rambow right away. His fleece was brighter, and he was a head taller than the rest of the flock. He looked mean just chewing his cud.

Psyche sang as she approached: *"Baa-baa Rambow, have you any wool?"*

Rambow turned toward her. His nostrils flared as he began making a terrible half-bleating, half-growling sound.

Psyche stopped singing. "Nice Rambow?"

Now the whole flock turned toward Psyche. They pawed the ground, their ears flattened menacingly on their woolly heads. And then, with a loud communal bleat, the flock charged Psyche.

"Hey! No! Stop!" she cried.

But on the sheep thundered, straight toward the hapless mortal.

"Yikes!" Psyche turned and started running up the hill through the thorns and briars. The sheep, which had thick wool to protect them, quickly gained on her. About halfway up the hill, the lead sheep were so close they were nipping at her heels. Psyche turned suddenly and ran back down the hill toward the river. She really put on some speed.

The sheep turned and charged after her. They chased her down the hill to the river's edge. Psyche didn't slow down, but plunged straight into the water. She swam to the middle of the river before she dared look over her shoulder to see if the sheep were swimming after her. But the flock had stopped at the river's edge. They stomped their hooves, bleating menacingly.

"Nice flock!" Psyche called, treading water. "I only want a few clippings of fleece."

Psyche was out of immediate danger, but she wasn't even close to completing her task. Helios's sun chariot was high in the sky now. Time was running out. I had to step in.

I quickly shifted into CCC. *Rambow?* I thought. *Do you read me, Rambow?*

Loud and clear, came the answer. *Who's asking?*

It's . . . uh, I didn't really want to say. This was Zeus's flock, after all. If Rambow ratted on me to Zeus, Aphrodite could find out about it, and Psyche would be out of luck.

It's me, uh, Flockio, I thought-beamed to Rambow. *Immortal protector of sheep.*

No kidding? Rambow thought back. *There's a sheep god?*

More or less. So, Rambow, I've come to ask you to give the poor mortal in the river there a break.

Why should we? Did you hear what she wants? My golden wool!

Well, give her some. After all, you shear a little off, it grows back.

Our wool is for Zeus, Rambow thought-beamed my way. *He makes us pay for grazing in his field by giving him our golden wool.*

Zeus charged his own sheep rent? How low could that god go?

Zeus wouldn't have to know, I thought to the lead sheep. *Say, Rambow, what do you and your flock like to graze on most of all?*

That's easy. Blue thistle. It's delicious! But very rare. There isn't any here.

What if I fixed it so that this whole meadow sprang up with blue thistle?

You could do that?

Am I the god of sheep, or what? Of course I can! Give the mortal a big pile of your wool, Rambow. And in a day or two, this whole meadow will be sprouting your favorite snack.

You've got a deal, Flockio! Rambow bleated to his flock. They turned suddenly from the river and huddled around their leader. After a moment, they walked over to the grass, lay down and closed their eyes.

Psyche saw this. Slowly and quietly, she swam toward the shore. She waded out of the river and tiptoed toward the apparently sleeping sheep. Singing softly, she took the golden shears and began shearing Rambow's wool:

"'Baa-baa Rambow, have you any wool?'
'Yes, Psyche! Yes, Psyche! Three bags full.'
'May I snip some wool, sir?' the hopeful Psyche asked.
'To give Aphrodite and so complete this task?'"

During the musical shearing, I walked down the riverbank a little way and called Persephone. "Hello, Phoney honey!" I said when she answered. "I need a couple of favors."

Persephone said no problem for the blue thistle. She said she'd always wanted to plant a great meadow of it. But she wasn't all that happy to hear the request for more strawberries.

"Every garden on Earth will be swarming with ants!" she said. "But all right, Hades. For you, I'll do it."

"Thanks P-phone," I said. "You're the best!"

By the time we hung up, Psyche had sheared a huge pile of Rambow's wool. She stuffed it into the collecting bag and drew up the strings. I hurried invisibly back in time to hear Psyche's last words to the sheep.

"I thank you with all my heart, golden sheep," Psyche said. Then she began the climb back up the hill. On her way, she saw that when the sheep had run through the bushes, tufts of their fleece had stuck on the thorns. So, as she climbed, she gathered clump after clump of golden fleece from the thorns. She made a pocket with the hem of her robe to hold the wool. By the time she reached the top of the hill, she had a second big bundle of fleece.

Helios was driving his sun chariot far to the west as Psyche ran back to Thunder Court.

Invisible nymphs opened the gate and let her in, and she hurried into the palace with her golden burden. Naturally, I wasn't far behind. Psyche ran through the palace to Cupid's room.

"Aphrodite!" Psyche called, knocking on the sick-room door. "I have completed the task!"

The door flew open. "*Imbecille!*" Aphrodite whispered. "Not so loud. You'll wake up *mio bambino*!" The goddess of L&B stepped out into the hallway and shut the door behind her.

"Here is the bag of Rambow's golden fleece," said Psyche, handing it to Aphrodite along with her shears. "It will make a fine blanket for Cupid." She untied the hem of her robe and gave Aphrodite the fleece she had collected coming up the hill. "With this you could make a soft pillow for Cupid's head."

Aphrodite's eyes widened as she saw so much golden wool. "*E tutto?* That's all?" she said, nearly choking on her words. "I expected more. But from you, I must learn to expect less."

Then Aphrodite's eyes flicked over the many little cuts on Psyche's arms and legs and face. She smiled.

But even though Psyche's hair was tangled, her robe was smeared with sheep grease, and her skin was red with welts, she was proving to be one of those rare mortals who just keeps looking better with each hardship. If Aphrodite's next task was to enter Psyche in a mud-wrestling tournament, Psyche would come out of it covered in mud and looking more beautiful than ever.

"Any week-old *bambino* could do these *piccolo*, little, tasks," said Aphrodite. "But now I have some *real* tasks for you."

"Give them to me," said Psyche. "I'm warmed up now."

Chapter XIII

Prisoner of Love

The next morning, unseen, I watched as Aphrodite handed Psyche a list. "These tasks you must complete if ever you wish to see *Cupidino* again," she said. "Now, *vai via*! Be gone! Don't knock on my door until you've finished every task. I have no wish to see your unfortunate face again soon. Oh, how it hurts my *bella* blue eyes to look at you!"

Psyche stared at the list. I read it over her shoulder.

Psyche's Tasks:

1. *Bring me a bar of Moon Goddess **sapone**, soap, from the Land of the Hyperborians, so that I may bathe my **Cupidino**.*

2. Bring me Pegasus, the flying steed, so he may flap his mighty wings and dry ***il mio bambino***.

3. Bring me some magic salve from the Nymphs of the North to soothe my ***Cupidino's*** wound.

4. Bring me an egg from the nest of the eagle of Seriphos so that I may make ***una frittata***, an omelet, for my son.

5. Bring me ***il pane,*** bread, from Dodona so that I may toast it for my ***Cupidino.***

6. Bring me ambrosia-milk from the fairy goats that graze on Mount Ida so that I may give my ***Cupidino*** a drink.

7. Bring me one of ***le fiore***, the flowers, that grow atop Mount Etna in Sicily so that its scent may cheer my boy.

8. Bring me the Calydonian Boar's softest bristle so that I may use it to tickle my ***Cupidino*** and make him laugh.

9. Bring me a box of yellow smoke from the oracle at Delphi so that I may ask it whether ***il mio bambino*** shall ever be healed.

10. *Bring me* ***una tazz,*** *a cup, of sea foam from the ocean waves that break on the shores of Cythera, just because I said so.*

These tasks would take Psyche to the end of the earth and back again. It would take her years and years to complete them. And since Psyche was a mortal, she didn't have all that many years.

Psyche looked up from the list. "When I bring you the ten items on this list, then will you forgive me for wounding Cupid? Then can I see him again?"

"*Certo!* Of course!" said the goddess of L&B. "If you bring them. It is a *grande if.*"

"Thank you, Aphrodite," Psyche said bravely. "I will go now. When I have finished my tasks, I will come back to Thunder Court and knock on your door."

"Don't come to me unless all the tasks are *finite,* finished!" said Aphrodite. Then, with a smile, she added, "You know, I think I will never see you again."

"May . . . may I tell Cupid goodbye before I go?" Psyche asked.

"*Tre* guesses," said Aphrodite. "And the first *due* don't count. *Vai via!* Go away!"

Psyche turned and ran down the hall to her room. Naturally, I rushed after her. She quickly packed up her few things, then hurried out the Thunder Court gates and rang the gong for Zephyr. *Bong!*

I stepped up next to her. "Hey, Psyche," I said, taking off my helmet. *FOOP!*

"Oh, Hades," she said. "Guess what? You were right! Aphrodite gave me a few tasks to do, and when I finish them, I can see Cupid again!"

Talk about a positive outlook! Psyche was totally pumped up and ready to do the impossible tasks. I hardly knew what to say.

"Great," I managed. "Did you, um, read the list of tasks?"

Psyche nodded. "Some of them will take a while," she admitted, making what I thought might be the understatement of all time. "But knowing that I'll see Cupid at the end makes them easy to face. Hey, the wind is picking up. Do you think it's Zephyr?"

"Of course it's me," said Zephyr. "Who else could Zeus get to shuttle gods and whatnot back and forth from this place, Pegasus?"

"Pegasus!" said Psyche as the West Wind picked us up and began blowing us back east. "He's on my list! Do you know where Pegasus lives, Zephyr?"

"I know all sorts of things," Zephyr said. "Not that I get any credit. Pegasus lives way north in the Land of the Hyberborians."

"Can you blow me there, Zephyr?" asked Psyche.

"It's halfway across the world," said Zephyr. "A two-day gust. I can take you there, no problem for this old wind. But you'll have to get home on your own. Zeus doesn't like it if his shuttle service is away for too long."

"Thank you, Zephyr!" said Psyche.

"Don't thank me," Zephyr said. "Nobody does."

"While you're in the Land of Hyperborians,"

I said, "ask Medusa to give you a bar of Moon Goddess soap. That'll save you a trip back there again."

Psyche and I talked as Zephyr blew us over the earth. The trip seemed to take hardly any time at all. Soon Zephyr called out, "Next stop, Craggy Peak!"

"Thanks, Zephyr!" I said as she gusted lower to drop me off. "Good luck, Psyche!"

"Thanks, Hades," said Psyche. "For everything. You've been a big help."

Little did she know!

And with a whoosh, Zephyr and Psyche were gone.

I quickly chanted the astro-traveling spell and zipped to Phaeton's Garage. There, I hitched up Harley and Davidson and headed for home.

Was I ever happy to be back at good ol' Villa Pluto. But I couldn't stay long. Two days later, I headed to the Land of Hyperborians to help Psyche complete one of her tasks. And that's how it went for the next couple of years. The Furies were a big help. They kept watch over Psyche as she wandered the earth to carry out her tasks. Whenever she neared a task site, Tisi let me know, and I showed up just before she got there to smooth her way. Well, showed up isn't exactly right. I always wore my helmet, so Psyche never knew that I was anywhere around.

But I was there to convince the Nymphs of the North to give her a jar of salve. I was at Seriphos to talk the Eagle into parting with one of her eggs. Dodona is my least favorite place in the universe, filled as it is with oaks who speak the will of Zeus. But Psyche needed a loaf of Dodona bread, and I was there to make sure she got it. I went to Mount Ida, too, the childhood home of Zeus, to see that Psyche got the fairy goat's ambrosia-milk. And when she showed up at the top of Mount Etna to pluck that flower, I was invisibly at her side.

After she got each item on the list, Psyche went to Craggy Peak and called Zephyr. The West Wind blew the item to Thunder Court and put it in the barn to wait until Psyche came back to knock on Aphrodite's door. Except for Pegasus. With only minor puffs from Zephyr, she rode the wild, winged horse to Thunder Court herself. She was truly a fearless mortal!

After Psyche got the rose from Mount Etna, she headed for Calydon to get the bristle from Boar. I knew it would take her weeks to get there, so I had some time. I called Zephyr myself, and asked her to blow me to Thunder Court. I wanted to check on Cupid.

The Wind put me down beside the palace. I put on my helmet — *POOF!* — and made my invisible way to Cupid's room. Aphrodite wasn't anywhere in sight. Good! I turned the knob and slowly opened the door.

"Hello?" called Cupid from where he sat in his bed. He wore pink satin pajamas with a red heart on the pocket. And green pimple goo all over his face. "Who's there?"

"Shhh!" I cautioned him, as I took off my helmet and — *FOOP!* — reappeared.

"Hades!" Cupid jumped up. "You gotta help me, man! My mom's holding me prisoner! She's fixed the lock so that I can't open the door from the inside. I'm trapped!"

"Where is your mother?" I asked.

"Primping in her dressing room," said Cupid. "Or maybe in her office."

"Her office?" I said.

"Yeah," said Cupid. "She's running her cosmetics empire from here. She'll do anything to keep me from getting loose and trying to find Psyche." Cupid rolled his eyes. "As if!"

"What do you mean?" I asked him. "Don't you want to see Psyche?"

"Of course I do!" said Cupid. "I miss her so much I can hardly stand it. But no way would I go looking for her. She doesn't want to see me, that's for sure."

"How do you know?" I asked.

"Big *duh*!" said Cupid. "She saw what I looked like and took off. I haven't heard from her since. Not a 'Hope Your Wound Is Better' card. Not a 'Hope It Didn't Leave a Scar' note. Nothing! She's probably married to some mortal by now. But so what? She'd never go for anyone who looked like me anyway."

I sat down on the foot of Cupid's bed and told him how his mom wouldn't let Psyche in to see him. I told him how she'd been traveling the world, doing nearly impossible tasks so she could see him again. I told him how she'd nearly been trampled by Zeus's killer sheep. How she'd ridden Pegasus, a wild, winged stallion, all the way to Thunder Court. I told him how the eagle of Seriphos had nearly pecked out her eyes.

"And now she's off getting a bristle from the Calydonian Boar," I said. "She's risking her short little mortal life day after day, and all for you. Doesn't that tell you something, Cupid?"

The parts of Cupid's face that weren't slathered with green goo were blushing as red as the heart on his pajama pocket.

"That's awesome!" said Cupid. "But you're not just saying that, are you, man?"

I shook my head. "But don't tell your mother I told you all this. It'll ruin everything."

"I'm not that dumb," said Cupid.

"Psyche has only three more tasks to complete," I added. "Then she can come and see you." I stood up to go. "The door's open now, Cupid. Why don't you escape?"

“I can’t!” said Cupid. “Mom’s hidden my robes. All I’ve got are these awful pjs!”

“I’ve seen worse,” I said, thinking of the black pajamas with orange flames Persephone had given me last Bacchus Day.

“Besides,” Cupid added, “I’ve still got pimples and braces and all.”

I wished Cupid would just fly out the door to freedom, but clearly he wasn’t ready yet.

“I’ll come check on you in a couple of weeks,” I said as I put on my helmet. *POOF!*

“Hades!” Cupid called as I left his room. “Thanks for everything. You are the dude, man!”

Chapter XIV

Kiss and Make Up?

I made my invisible way across the courtyard. I sniffed. What was that awful smell? It was coming from the pink marble goat shed. My question was answered by Grub appearing at the shed door, yawning and scratching his belly. He trotted over to Cupid's window and shouted, "Grub need food!"

Cupid stuck his head out the window. "Keep your robe on, man!" he called down to Grub. "I told you, Zephyr's bringing it!"

"Grub hungry now!" called the goatherd.

Just then the wind picked up, and a package floated through the air toward Grub. His face lit up as he reached out to take it.

"There you go, stinky pants," said Zephyr. "That'll keep you fed for a day or two."

"Hey, Zephyr!" I called. "Any chance I can catch a ride to Calydon?"

"Why not?" said the Wind, lifting me in a swirling gust. "Got nothing else to do."

When I arrived, I headed straight to the Calydonian Boar's Championship Wrestling School. The place was packed with little pigs hoping to make it big on the wrestling circuit. I found Boar working out with his trainer. I complimented his Flying-Hoof Thrust — I felt like such a traitor to Eagle-Eye! — and Boar agreed to pluck out his softest bristle and give it to Psyche when she showed up.

A few weeks later, I went to Delphi to make sure that my Granny Gaia would have plenty of yellow smoke rising the day Psyche got to the oracle. When the Furies told me Psyche had boarded a ship bound for Cythera, I astro-traveled to the island. When I got there, I saw Psyche standing knee-deep in the surf. She dipped her cup into the sea and brought it up filled with foam. She put a lid on it and placed it in her bag.

"Yes!" cried Psyche. "My last task is finished. *Finito!* Now I can go back to Aphrodite in victory. Now she will see that I love Cupid with all my heart." She took out her harmonica and played a sort of haunting melody. Then she began to sing:

"My heart belongs to Cupid.
There are some who may think it odd,
But my heart belongs to Cupid.
I'm a mortal in love with a god."

This didn't sound like Psyche's usual silly songs. It was a little sad, and seemed to come straight from her soul.

Psyche waded to shore and started her journey back to Craggy Peak. I smiled as I watched her go. In a few weeks she would show her items to Aphrodite. The goddess of L&B would be flabbergasted that Psyche had managed to get everything on her list. But she couldn't help but admire Psyche's doggedness. But would she let Cupid and Psyche be together again? She'd said, "*Certo!* Of course!" She'd given her word. And when she saw how much Cupid and Psyche loved each other, surely she wouldn't try any of her tricks.

Having seen Psyche through her ten tasks, I was glad to take up my old routine in the Underworld. Time went by. Persephone came home each winter and went back up to earth each spring. For a couple of years, I was too busy to make it up to Wrestle Dome. But whenever I tuned into one of Cyclops's matches on TV, I always thought of King Otis. I hadn't heard a word from Cupid or Psyche, but I took that as a good sign. When Persephone and I first fell in love, the last thing we thought about was keeping in touch with our friends.

Then, one evening, near the end of a winter, Persephone and I were sitting down to dinner when the doorbell rang.

"I'm not expecting anyone," said Persephone. "Are you, Hades?"

"Not me," I said.

I heard the front door open. Footsteps sounded on the stone floor of Villa Pluto, and

Hypnos, my first lieutenant, poked his head into the dining room.

"Excuse me for interrupting your dinner," said Hypnos. "But, well, this is most unusual. You know Cerberus has never let a mortal cross into your Underworld Kingdom — until tonight."

I jumped up. "Is Cerbie hurt?" That was the only reason I could think of that the dog would let a mortal pass through the Gates of the Underworld without ripping him to pieces.

"Not at all," said Hypnos. "May I show the mortal in?"

"Yes, yes," I said, still worried about Cerberus. This was unheard of.

Cerbie bounded into the dining room, wagging his whole rear end with happiness. I was alarmed. When the two of us were alone, Cerberus sometimes showed me his silly side, but he always took his Guardian of the Gates duties very seriously.

Then, to my utter astonishment, into our dining room walked Psyche. She looked older now, the way mortals always do when you haven't seen them for a few years. But she was more beautiful than ever. Her beauty was different from what it had been — it seemed to come from somewhere deep inside. And why did she look so tired and worn?

"Hello, Hades," she said. "Queen Persephone." She bowed toward Persephone.

"So, you're Psyche," said Persephone. "Oh, you are just as beautiful as Hades always said. Sit down! You look as if you've had a hard journey. Did you walk all the way here?"

Psyche nodded. "It took me nine days and nine nights," she said. "But that's not bad compared to some of the treks I've made."

"And Cerberus, my guard dog," I said. "How did you get past him?"

Psyche smiled. "At first he was very fierce," she said.

Cerbie bared all three sets of his teeth, as if to show his ferocious side.

"I had a bit of cake with me," Psyche said, "so I gave him some, and we became friends."

Now Cerbie wagged his stumpy tail, as if demonstrating his friendly nature.

"Cake?" I said. "That's all it took, eh, Cerbie?" I patted his heads. "Yes, you're a good dog. You know who to let inside my gates."

Hypnos came in carrying a plate of food for Psyche. I saw that he'd thoughtfully left the ambrosia sauce off her pasta, and had substituted plain tomato sauce instead. He knew better than to serve a mortal the food of the gods. If mortals eat ambrosia and drink nectar, then they'll become immortal, too — and wouldn't that be a mess!

Psyche really dug into her pasta.

"What has brought you down to see us, Psyche?" Persephone asked as she ate.

"Two of Aphrodite's tasks," answered Psyche.

"Tasks?" I exclaimed. "But you finished your tasks."

"I finished the first ten," Psyche told me. "Then I went to see Aphrodite. I gave her everything on her list."

"Then she let you see Cupid, right?" I said.

Psyche sadly shook her head. "Aphrodite hardly looked at what I had brought her. She just handed me another list."

"What?" I cried. "More tasks? But Aphrodite gave her word that you could see Cupid when you finished that first list."

Psyche shrugged, as if to say there was no explaining Aphrodite. "She gave me lots more tasks. They were much harder than the first ten."

"But how did you do them without . . . I mean . . . I am so glad you were able to do these tasks," I said. Had Psyche really accomplished these difficult tasks on her own? Without my help? It was hard to believe.

Psyche nodded. "I finished the tasks on the second list, but when I went to see Aphrodite, the same thing happened. So now I need two things from the Underworld to complete my third list."

Three lists! Aphrodite was truly cruel!

"What do you need, dear?" asked Persephone.

"Aphrodite wants a cup of water from the River Styx," said Psyche. "So she can swear on it always to care for Cupid. I dipped a cup in the river while the ferryman brought me over to the Underworld, so I have the water. But I need something from you, Queen Persephone."

"Name it," said Persephone. "It's yours."

"Aphrodite says tending Cupid for so long has taken a toll on her beauty," said Psyche.

"What?" I cried. "Surely she can't *still* be nursing that boy! Why, it's been years since the, er . . . the accident," I said, taking care to spare Psyche's feelings. "I saw Cupid's wound. It was nothing that a good cleaning and a bandage couldn't have fixed up in a week."

Psyche reached into her bundle and drew out a box. She handed it to Persephone. "Aphrodite asks that you fill this with some of your makeup, Queen Persephone. Aphrodite says she wants to use it to recapture her own beauty."

"Oh, for Mount Olympus's sakes!" said Persephone. "Aphrodite has some nerve!"

Psyche nodded sadly. "I understand," she said, reaching out to take back the box. "Not every goddess is happy to share the secrets of her beauty."

"That's not it!" said Persephone. "Aphrodite is the beauty-products expert. Her potions are sold in all the best stores in Athens and Thebes. Even

Olympians use them on the sly. She has seven different lines of products." She began counting on her fingers. "Aphrodite Basic, Aphrodite Lite, Aphrodite Look-in-the-Mirror, Aphrodite Forever, Aphrodite Future, Aphrodite Ooh-La-La, and — what's the name of that really pricy Italian line, Hades? Oh, I know. Bella Venus Ultra."

Psyche sighed. "Sometimes Aphrodite puts items on the lists just to amuse herself. I guess this is one of them."

"I spend about two minutes a day on makeup," said Persephone. "But it's probably best to give Aphrodite what she wants. I'll go fill this up." And she hurried off to her powder room."

"Has Aphrodite ever let you see Cupid?" I asked.

Psyche shook her head. "Not yet. But once I have Persephone's box of beauty, I can knock on Aphrodite's door once more and give her all that she has asked for. This time she might let me see him." Psyche began singing softly,

"I can't love another,
For me, there's no other,
So tell me, what else can I do?
I'd rather search the whole world through,
From the Underworld to Olympus above . . .
Than give up my little god of love."

I listened, stunned by what I was hearing. Psyche took out her harmonica and played the tune she'd just sung. Persephone stood in the doorway listening too. When Psyche finished, I knew I had to take action. Psyche had suffered enough for love.

Persephone drew her chair next to Psyche's. "Here you go, Psyche." She flipped up the lid of the box. "See? I've put in blush, lipstick, eye shadow, and mascara."

"Thank you, Queen Persephone." Psyche smiled. Then she closed the lid and put the box into her bundle. She got up. "The sooner I go, the sooner I'll get to see Cupid. Thank you both so much." She bent down to pat Cerberus. "You, too, pup. Bye-bye!"

Cerbie gave her hand the old triple licking. I'd never seen him take to anyone the way he had to Psyche. I'd have to find out where she got that cake.

"Wait, Psyche," I said. "You're in no shape to start out on a nine-day hike."

"Hades is right," said Persephone. "Stay the night here in Villa Pluto, and Hades can drive you up to Earth tomorrow morning."

Psyche looked unsure. "But I gave my word to complete the tasks on my own. Without any help from any god."

"Has Aphrodite kept her word?" I asked.

Psyche shook her head.

"You've got the box of beauty," I told her. "You did that on your own. Besides, you didn't ask for help. I offered. It will be fine if I give you a lift back up to Earth."

"And you'll get to see Cupid eight days sooner," said Persephone.

Psyche smiled. "I'm staying!"

Persephone took her to the Furies' wing of the palace and settled her in the guest room. Then she came back into the dining room.

"That poor mortal!" Persephone said. "We have to do something to help her, Hades."

"You're right," I said. "This can't go on. Psyche is growing weak. Not to mention getting older."

"Why doesn't Cupid fly away from Thunder Court?" asked Persephone. "A locked door never kept in any god who wanted to be free."

"I know," I told her. "Cupid blames it on his pajamas. But I think he feels bad about the way he looks. He still can't believe Psyche could love him back."

Hypnos brought us two ambrosia-foam cappuccinos. We sipped them beside a roaring fire and plotted how we might put an end to Aphrodite's torment — and find a way to bring Cupid and Psyche together again. By the time our fire had burned down to coals, we'd come up with a plan.

Minutes later, Persephone, Hypnos, and I were hurrying to the guest room. Slowly, slowly, Hypnos opened the guest room and tossed in a few grains of sleep sand to make Psyche fall into a deep slumber. Poor mortal. She looked as if she needed a good night's rest.

When Hypnos gave the nod that Psyche was asleep, Persephone tiptoed into her room. She picked up her bundle, took out the box, and tiptoed out again. I opened the box and dumped out all the makeup. Then I slipped something else entirely into the box and closed the lid. I made sure the latch fit tight. Then Persephone took the box, crept back into Psyche's room, and put it into her bundle. When she came out again, Hypnos quietly closed the door behind us.

Outside in the hallway, the three of us slapped hands.

"Yes!" said Persephone. "This is going to be *good*!"

Chapter XV

Nice Shot, Hades!

"Let's go, Harley! Come on, Davidson!" I called to my steeds. "Let's hit the road!"

The road was the rocky, bumpy, curvy Underworld Highway. I drove my SUV chariot that day. Persephone sat up front with me, and Psyche sat in the back with Cerbie. We made it up to earth that day in less than two hours, and a short time later we pulled into a parking lot in Thebes. After I settled my steeds, I picked up Psyche, Persephone picked up Cerberus, and the four of us quickly astro-traveled to the top of Craggy Peak.

"Wow!" said Psyche when we landed and I put her down. "That sure beats walking all over the world."

Persephone put Cerbie down. "How do we call the West Wind, Hades?"

"No need to call today!" said a raspy voice. "Zephyr is here, at your beck and call. Yep, you can count on the good ol' West Wind to show up every time. Got nothing better to do."

"Ah, there you are, Zephyr," I said to the swirling air.

"Hi, Zephyr!" said Psyche. "I'm back again!"

"So I see," said Zephyr. "Just can't stay away from Cupid's mother, can you? She reminds me of my mother, Agusta. She's liked North Wind best, ever since he was just a little puff. Always had time for South Wind, too. But did she have time for West Wind? Ha!"

"Zephyr," I said. "Can we talk for a minute? In private?"

"No problem." Zephyr picked me up and took me off a few hundred dekafeet down the hill. "You want to ask another favor, am I right? Why else would you want to talk to me?"

"It's a huge favor, Zephyr," I told the Wind. "And I'll be grateful to you for all my days —

which is basically forever — if you'll help me out here." And I explained the plan that Persephone and I had cooked up the night before. "Can you do that, Zephyr?" I asked. "Can you?"

"Of course I *can*," the Wind said. "Nothing to it. But will I?" The Wind picked me up again and spun me around so fast that I got dizzy. She twirled me back to where the others were waiting. "You'll have to wait and see!"

Then Zephyr picked up the lot of us and blew us to Thunder Court.

"Some swanky hideaway," Persephone said as the palace and grounds came into view.

"Persephone," I whispered. "Look — Psyche's fallen asleep."

The exhausted mortal lay peacefully in the arms of the West Wind.

"No wonder," said Zephyr. "This kid logs about a thousand dekamiles a week going places for the so-called goddess of love. Here, I'll put the rest of you down and take Psyche on to the stable. She can sleep on the hay. Wouldn't be the first time I've done it."

"That's nice, Zephyr," I said. "Thanks for the ride."

The Wind lowered Persephone, Cerberus, and me to the ground just inside the gate. We watched then as Psyche seemed to float over the courtyard and into the stable.

The quiet was broken by Cerberus growling. *"Grrrrrr! Grrrrrr! Grrrrrr!"*

"What's wrong, pooch?" I asked.

"It's that big dog, Hades," said Persephone, pointing. "Look!"

"Oh, T-Bolt!" I said. "She's only got one head, Cerbie. She's no threat."

But Cerberus kept growling.

"You'd better get going, Hades," said Persephone. "I'll stay here and hold Cerbie." It was a generous offer, because Persephone wasn't all that big on our dog.

"Right," I said. "Thanks, P-phone." And I strode purposefully toward the palace.

T-Bolt was crouched down in front of her doggie palace, growling. With these two dogs, it was hate at first sight. I hurried into the palace and put on my helmet. *POOF!* I went straight to Cupid's room. I slowly opened the door. Luckily, Aphrodite didn't seem to be around.

Cupid was sitting up in bed, reading a book. I glanced at the title: *From Scrawny to Brawny in Just X Days!* He had on a truly embarrassing pair of pajamas. They were white with giant red hearts all over. Inside each heart, letters spelled out **I LOVE MY MOMMY!** His face was smeared with bright green pimple cream.

Cupid looked up. His eyes grew wide as he saw the door open.

"Hades?" he whispered. "Is that you?"

"It is," I said, removing my helmet. *FOOP!* I looked at Cupid, frowning.

"What's wrong?" said Cupid.

"What's on your forehead?" I asked.

"What, the zit cream?"

"No, it's something else. Some sort of growth."

"Oh, man! What now?" Cupid raced over to his mirror. He examined his forehead. "I don't see anything, Hades."

"Up by the hairline," I told him. "Maybe you can't see it because of the cream."

He grabbed one of his cast-off pajama tops and began wiping the green goo off his face.

As he concentrated on his image in the mirror, I took a small arrow from my pocket. One of Cupid's arrows. I didn't bother with the bow. I walked up behind him and stuck him in the back of the neck — exactly the spot where he'd hit me a few hundred years ago.

"OW!" Cupid yelled. "Hey, Hades! What's going —"

Cupid stopped talking. He stared at himself in the mirror. "Oh, wow!" he cried, continuing to stare. "Who's that totally handsome dude staring back at me, man?"

"It's you, Cupid. It's you." I smiled and congratulated myself. "Nice shot, Hades!"

Chapter XVI

Zing! Zing! Zing!

"Come on, Cupid," I said. "The door's open. Let's go outside."

"No, man," said Cupid, smiling giddily at himself in the mirror. "I'm happy here."

I stepped in front of the little god of love, took hold of the mirror frame, and yanked. With a loud crunching noise, the mirror came off the wall.

"Here," I said, handing it to Cupid. "Now, let's go."

Cupid held the mirror, gazing at himself, while I led him down the stairs and out of the palace so he wouldn't trip over his own feet. In the courtyard, he glanced around briefly. Then his gaze dropped lovingly back to the mirror.

I propped him up against a pillar, where he seemed content to stand, admiring himself.

I ran across the courtyard and gave a quick thumbs-up to Persephone, who was sitting under a shade tree, holding Cerbie by the collar. I ran to the gong, picked up the mallet and started banging. *BONG! BONG! BONG!* I hoped everyone at Thunder Court would run outside.

To my astonishment, Muffy and Buffy ran out of the pink marble laundry cottage.

"What are you doing here?" I asked when they ran over to see what was happening. "I thought Zephyr took you home years ago!"

"She wouldn't take us," said Muffy.

"She said we were the rudest mortals she'd ever met," said Buffy.

"We don't mind," said Muffy. "We like it here with invisible servants to wait on us."

"What's going on, anyway?" asked Buffy. "Why are you banging on the gong?"

"You'll see." I kept banging. Now Grub ran out of the goat shed, followed by all the goats.

"Woke up Grub!" grunted the smelly mortal.

"Ewwww!" Stay away from us, Grub!" shrieked Muffy.

"Far away!" screamed Buffy.

Next, Psyche stumbled out of the barn, only half awake, her bundle on her shoulder. She seemed even more surprised than I was to see her sisters.

Finally, Aphrodite hurried out the palace door. "*Mamma mia!*" she cried. She lifted a hand to shield her eyes from the sun. "*Pluto?*" she said. "Is that you making all this racket?"

It took me a moment to figure out that she meant me, Hades. "It is," I answered.

"What in *il mondo* is going on —" she stopped suddenly, catching sight of Psyche. "You!" she screeched. "Did I not tell you to stay away until every task on that list was *finito*?"

"They are all *finito*," said Psyche. "I have brought you every item on the third list."

Aphrodite frowned. "What about the box of *la bellezza*, beauty, from Persephone? You never got that, did you? Mortals cannot enter the Underworld!"

"I have it here!" said Psyche. She pulled the box from her bag and held it out to Aphrodite. "All the tasks are complete."

"On *that* list maybe," said Aphrodite. She took the box, and her fingers worked to open the latch. "But I've got another list of tasks for you. This one's *twice* as long as —" she lifted the lid of the box. "*Imbecille!*" she cried. "This is not *la bellezza*!"

"But it must be!" said Psyche in distress. "Persephone showed me the blush, lipstick, and eye shadow!"

"*Guardi!* Look!" Aphrodite cried, thrusting the box into Psyche's face. "This box is full of arrows!" As the words left her mouth, a crazy wind whirled through the courtyard. It picked up the arrows from the box and flung them this way and that way, scattering them in all directions.

A chorus of cries sounded as the tiny arrows found their marks.

"Ow!"

"Ouch!"

"I'm zinged!"

"Ooch!"

"Ye, gods!"

"Owwwwwwwww!"

Persephone and I grinned at each other.

"You told Zephyr not to zing Cupid or Psyche, didn't you, Hades?" said Persephone.

I nodded. Our plan was working perfectly!

Everyone ran in circles. No one knew what was going on. It was as if Pan had given one of his earsplitting screams and sent everyone into a panic. At last the arrows stopped flying. The gods and mortals and dogs and goats stopped running, and peace settled on the courtyard.

Aphrodite shattered it with a cry. "Oh, *il mio mortalino*!" She rushed down the palace steps toward Grub. "*Che bello!* How handsome you are. And —" She took a long sniff. "Ah! You smell like sweet *profumo*!"

Grub stared at the goddess of L&B in disbelief.

Aphrodite threw her arms wide. "Let me embrace you!" she cried. "For I love you with all my heart, *mi amore*!"

Now Grub's eyes lit up. "Yes, nice goddess, come to Grub!"

"No, Grub!" cried Muffy, hurrying over to the goatherd. "Say you'll be my man!"

"No, mine!" cried Buffy, elbowing her sister out of the way. "I saw him first!"

Aphrodite aimed a couple of her power kicks at the twins, and the mortals backed off.

"*Per favore*, give me *un bacio*, a kiss!" Aphrodite threw her arms around Grub's neck.

Grub obeyed.

"Now I want a kiss!" said Muffy.

"Oh, boy!" Grub said. "Everybody love Grub!"

"Not everybody, man!" said Cupid as he walked down the palace steps holding the mirror up in front of his face. "For I know someone who is in love with Cupid."

"I am!" shouted Psyche, running toward the little god of love. "Oh, Cupid! At last you understand that I love you!"

Cupid looked up at Psyche, smiling in surprise. "Well, that makes two of us," he said. "For I love me, too!"

"What?" said Psyche.

"I love me!" cried Cupid. "With all my heart."

At the other side of the courtyard, a tussle broke out. Muffy and Buffy were pulling on one of Grub's arms, while Aphrodite had a firm grip on the other.

"Wait!" Grub cried. "Don't break Grub! Stop! Take turns!"

"I knew our plan would work," Persephone told me, laughing. "But I never imagined it would be this good!"

I smiled. "Hey, where's Cerbie? I thought he was with you."

"Over there." She gave a nod toward T-Bolt's dog palace.

Cerbie and T-Bolt were chasing each other, jumping and rolling happily on the grass.

"Aw, P-phone, they're in puppy love!" I said.

Persephone smiled, then grew suddenly serious. "You didn't put any red-tipped arrows in the box, did you, Hades?"

I shook my head. "No. Only orange. The potion will wear off in three days."

"Three days?" Persephone laughed and shook her head. "I hope they all survive!"

Now a gust of wind swept by us. "Don't thank me, Hades," Zephyr said. "I'd probably drop dead if anyone showed me any appreciation. If I carried out your plan, well, good. I hope you're happy. It's not what I do. I mean, how could one as unloved and unappreciated as the West Wind ever be happy? I don't know how —"

"Zephyr," I said. "Blow this whistle to the east for me, will you?" Then I put my thumb and first finger into my mouth and whistled loud and long.

The West Wind gusted and blew the whistle east. "There!" she said. "Another favor, done! You keep asking, and I keep doing. Even if I get no thanks. That's how it is."

"Do it again, Zephyr," I said and once more gave the series of whistles.

Zephyr blew them east again.

It wasn't long before the faint whir of flapping wings sounded in the distance.

"Thanks, Zephyr!" I said. "Now, keep swirling right where you are. Don't blow away!"

I ran across the courtyard to get Cupid. He

was lying on his back in the grass, holding the mirror up in front of his face, gazing lovingly at his reflection. Psyche sat beside him, looking lovingly down at him.

I took his bow out of my wallet. "Here, Cupid," I said, handing it to him. "And here's a couple of arrows. Orange ones. I need you to do some zinging."

"Later, man," said Cupid.

"Now, Cupid," I said, snatching away his mirror.

"Hey!" he cried. "Give that back!"

"The sooner you zing, the sooner you'll have it back," I told him. "Zing Orp," I said and pointed to the large six-winged serpent, who was flapping with all his might as he prepared to land.

"So that's Orp," said Psyche. "My supposed kidnapper."

Cupid jumped to his feet. He placed one of the orange-tipped arrows in his bow and took aim at Orp, who, with a great deal of flapping, had barely managed to skim over the courtyard wall.

ZING!

"Yikessssss!" cried Orp, as he landed. "Ssssssomething sssstuck me!"

"Nice shot, Cupid," I said. "Now zing Zephyr."

Cupid put in another arrow and fired it at a little tornado of dust swirling in the courtyard.

ZING!

"Yowie!" cried Zephyr. "Is this the thanks I get for —" She stopped talking as Orp skidded to a stop near the swirling dust. "Well, hello there, Mr. Serpent!" said Zephyr.

And suddenly Orp was swept up in a great rushing whoosh of wind and carried high into the sky.

"Oh, yessss!" cried the airborne serpent. "Now *thisssss* isssss sssssoaring!"

I smiled as I handed the mirror back to the little god of love. "Nice shot, Cupid!"

Chapter XVII

Love's Reward

Those were three wild days at Thunder Court. Zephyr flew off to who-knows-where with Orp, so no one could leave. I took Persephone to meet Queen Thorax, and Persephone promised her a bumper crop of strawberries. The two queens totally hit it off.

Then I took Persephone to meet Rambow. He and his herd were changed sheep ever since the crop of blue thistle had sprung up. They'd eaten their fill and were no more dangerous now than a pack of bunny rabbits.

In the late afternoon, the invisible nymphs set up tables on the palace porch. Persephone and I ordered a couple of nectar lattes and some snacks and sat there, watching the action.

Cerbie and T-Bolt were running around, chasing the goats all over the courtyard. Grub took turns receiving the attentions of Aphrodite, Muffy, and Buffy. And Cupid and Psyche? They talked for hours about how incredibly good-looking Cupid was. P-phone and I enjoyed the spectacle tremendously. But we were a little nervous about what would happen when the potions started wearing off.

Aphrodite was the first one to return to her non-zinged state. It was very sudden. One moment she was walking hand in hand with Grub through the rose gardens, and the next she was shrieking, "*Basta!* Let go of me, you smelly goat tender!" The mortified goddess ran up to her room and stayed there the rest of the day.

Grub wasn't upset. He simply took Muffy's hand and kept walking through the garden.

I knew Cupid had fallen out of love with himself when he came out to the porch for breakfast on the third morning. He wasn't carrying a mirror.

"Hey, Hades," he said as he passed me on

the way to the buffet. Then he caught sight of Psyche, sitting alone at a table, nibbling on a roll. The little god of love stood still as a statue, staring at Psyche, just as he had the first time he saw her. I knew what was going on. For the second time, it was love at first sight for Cupid.

When he was able to move again, Cupid rushed over to her table. He sat down across from her, took her hand, and looked into her eyes. "Psyche!" he said. "I love you."

Psyche had been waiting a long, *long* time for this moment. She looked back at him, smiling in all her radiant beauty.

The air was suddenly filled with clapping and whistling. I looked around. I didn't see anyone cheering. Then I realized it was the invisible nymphs. Maybe they couldn't speak. But they'd found a way to cheer for Cupid and Psyche.

Psyche jumped up from her seat and started singing,

"Oooooh, I feel great! That's what I wanted you to say now.

I feel great! I've been waiting for this day now.
Waiting just to hear three words, that might sound stupid,
But not when the one saying them is a god named Cupid.
Oooooh, I feel great! 'Cause don't you see now?
So great! 'Cause he's in love with me now!
Yow!"

The nymphs started clapping again. Cupid threw his arms around Psyche, and they clapped and whistled some more. But as the clapping died down, I heard a commotion in the courtyard. I turned to see what was going on. All the happiness I'd been feeling drained out of my godly body.

Zeus had just blown in.

"Who is this riffraff?" he bellowed, looking in horror at Grub, who was sitting on a garden bench between Muffy and Buffy, sharing their affections. "What's going on here?"

Then Zeus saw his vicious guard dog cavorting with Cerbie. "T-Bone! Get away from that mutt! You'll catch the mange!"

Zeus spotted me standing on the palace porch. "You, Hades? Here? This place really is going to the dogs."

Just then Zeus caught sight of Aphrodite looking down from a palace window. "Ye, gods! What's *she* doing here? I didn't marry her again, did I?"

"I don't think so," I told Zeus. Of course with him, you never knew for sure. "She came to get Cupid a few years ago and stuck around."

"Humph." Zeus suddenly looked stricken. "Hera isn't here, is she?"

"Haven't seen her," I said.

"I hope not," he said. "Came here to, uh, get away for a couple of days."

At that moment Grub, Muffy, and Buffy ran by, shrieking and playing a wild game of tag.

"Unsavory mortals? Here?" Zeus cried. He cupped his hands to his mouth and shouted, "Zephyr! Get over here now, Wind, on the double!"

"Hello again, Zeus!" Zephyr said. "Such a lovely day, isn't it?

"Who cares?" Zeus said. "Listen, get these mortals out of here! Whoosh them away. Disappear them from my sight on the double! Now, Zephyr!"

"Sure, Zeus," said Zephyr. "Always glad to help you out." And with that, she gusted down and swept Grub, Muffy, and Buffy into the air.

"We're leaving?" said Muffy as she floated away from Thunder Court.

"But the jewels!" said Buffy.

"Gone!" cried Grub mournfully.

And soon, they were.

The Zeus bellowed, "Cupid! Get out here, on the double! You are in big trouble!"

Cupid managed to tear his gaze from Psyche and run to the courtyard to meet his father. "Yo, dad!" he cried. "I have to talk to you!"

"I'll talk first," Zeus said. "Did I say you could have a party without me here? I did NOT!"

"It's not a party, Dad," said Cupid. "But guess what?"

"I don't do guessing games." Zeus began walking toward the palace.

"Psyche loves me, Dad!" said Cupid, trying to keep up with his dad. "For real! I didn't even zing her. And she doesn't care if I have braces. Or a few zits!"

"That's nice." Zeus climbed the steps onto the portico. "I want some lunch. Where are my serving nymphs? I don't see any of them around."

"You turned them invisible, Dad," said Cupid. "Listen, Psyche and I want to get married."

"What?" thundered Zeus. "You can't marry a mortal!"

"But you've done it, Dad," said Cupid. "Lots of times."

"That's different," said Zeus. "And that brings up a point I've been meaning to speak to you about, Cupid. I know most of my hasty weddings to mortals have been your fault. You shoot me with your love arrows, and I make a complete fool of myself! Why, you've forced me to turn into a bull, a swan, a shower of golden rain, and even a little bitty birdie. You've got to cut this out, Cupid. Do you hear me? I have my dignity to consider."

"Dignity?" Cupid rolled his eyes. "Sure, Dad."

"Now, where were we? Oh, yes, I'm your father, and I say you can't marry a mortal!" thundered Zeus.

"That's cool," said Cupid. "So make Psyche an immortal."

"Not a chance," said Zeus. "I can't just bestow immortality on some random mortal. It's a big deal. It's only for mortals who do great, heroic deeds."

"But Psyche has, Dad!" said Cupid.

"It's true, Zeus," I said. "She's completed dozens of nearly impossible tasks for Aphrodite. It took her years."

"Who asked you, Hades?" said Zeus. "I said no, and I'm sticking with that."

"Psyche even walked all the way to the Underworld," said Cupid. "It took her nine days and nights." He folded his arms across his chest. "Listen, Dad, I may be a little god, but I have my powers. If you want me to stop zinging you whenever I feel like it, then make Psyche immortal."

"What are you doing, standing up to your old man?" said Zeus.

"Exactly," said Cupid.

Zeus grinned. "That's my boy!" he said, slapping Cupid on the back. "About time, too. So, okay. If it makes you happy, I can make little what's-her-name immortal."

Just then little what's-her-name came down the palace steps. The King of the Universe took one look at the lovely mortal, and his mouth dropped open. He was thunderstruck.

"Psyche and I want to move up to Mount Olympus," Cupid said. "Maybe we could live in your palace until we get a place of our own."

Psyche smiled. "Are you really going to turn me into an immortal so I can marry Cupid?"

"Hey," said Zeus. "No problemo."

That night, Zeus held a banquet at Thunder Court. He sat at the head of his golden table with Cupid and Psyche on either side of him. Persephone and I sat next to them.

Aphrodite came late and slid into the chair at the way far end of the table. "*Buena sera,*" she mumbled, smiling weakly. She looked beautiful, of course, but strained. This whole episode with Grub had shaken her badly.

Invisible nymphs filled our golden goblets with nectar. Then Zeus stood up. He raised his goblet. "Ready to become an immortal, Psyche?" he said.

"*Cosa?* What?" cried Aphrodite, jumping to her feet. "Zeus, don't you dare!"

"Mom!" said Cupid. "Stop!"

"No!" Aphrodite held out her arms to Zeus. "*Prego,* Jupiter! Please! No! I sent Psyche off to do tasks. While she was away, the mortals on earth forgot about her. They came back to my temples. Soon they'll start sending me burnt offerings again. You think I want Psyche, this *cavolo,* running around earth *forever*?"

Psyche turned to Cupid. "What did your mom just call me?"

"Um, a cabbage," said Cupid.

"Down, Aphrodite!" said Zeus.

"No!" wailed Aphrodite. "Psyche will set up her own temples! She'll start her own line of products and fragrances! Maybe I'm losing my *il mio bambino* to her, but I'm not going to let her take over my *la bellezza* biz without a fight!" Aphrodite was pretty worked up.

I hurried over and yanked the goddess of L&B back down into her chair. "Cupid and Psyche want to live on Mount Olympus," I told her. "Psyche will go down to earth to visit her family once in a while. But not enough for mortals to worship or adore her."

"That's right," said Psyche. "I don't want that sort of attention." She turned to Cupid and smiled at him. "I just want to be with Cupid."

Aphrodite narrowed her eyes at the mortal she had gone to such pains to get rid of. "No ambitions for Psyche's soothing bubble bath? Or Psyche's stress-reducing aroma oil?"

"Never!" said Psyche.

Aphrodite smiled. "*Bene!* And you'll take good care of *il mio Cupidino*? Make nice soup for him, put on his pimple cream, iron his pajamas?"

"Mom!" cried Cupid. "Yuck! I don't want Psyche doing stuff like that."

Aphrodite turned to Psyche. "You look tired, *cara mia*. Come to my room after supper, and let me give you something for those dark circles under your eyes, *mia Psycelina*."

Psyche shrugged. "Why not?"

A smile spread slowly across Aphrodite's lips. "Ahhhh!" she said. "I'll take off for Mount Olympus first thing tomorrow. You know, I can almost smell the scent of burnt offerings right now!" She looked around at all of us happily. "*Mangia! Mangia!*" she said. "Let's eat!"

"First, a toast," said Cupid. "To Psyche!"

All of us gods and goddesses raised our goblets and drank down our nectar. Psyche looked at Cupid, then closed her eyes and did the same.

"Yum," said Psyche after she finished hers. "So now I'm immortal? Wow."

I took the last shish kebab from the platter. I needed to fuel up for the journey ahead of me. I was going to Thebes that night, to Wrestle

Dome, where Eagle-Eye had a rematch against Stinger. I planned to tell King Otis all that had happened to Psyche. Then the two of us would yell ourselves hoarse as we watched Eagle-Eye pin the Scorpion to the mat.

EPILOGUE

When I finally finished writing *Nice Shot, Cupid!*, I sent it over to my uncle Shiner. The Cyclops has an eye for a good story, and I wanted to get his feedback before sending it off to my publisher.

After I sent him the manuscript, I took my copy of *The Big Fat Book of Greek Myths* and went over to the Underworld Gym to work out the kinks in my neck. There's nothing worse for a god's neck — or a mortal's, either — than sitting at a desk all day, typing.

I was on the Neckersizer, reading through the myths, when I caught sight of Uncle Shiner striding toward me. He had my manuscript tucked under his arm.

"This is an excellent story, Hades," he said. "You have a good ear for dialogue."

"Thanks, Uncle Shiner!" I said.

"But I wonder if you ended the story too soon," Shiner added.

"You think?" I said.

A line had formed for the Neckersizer, so I let go of the straps, picked up my book, and led Uncle Shiner over to some benches. We sat down next to one another.

"I wanted to know whether Cupid and Psyche married," said Shiner.

"They did," I told the Cyclops. "After Psyche drank the nectar and became immortal, Zeus performed the ceremony. Psyche asked Persephone to be her bridesmaid, and Cupid asked me to be his best god. Zeus objected, of course. But Cupid had gotten the hang of standing up to his old dad, so I stood beside him at the altar."

"What about Aphrodite?" asked Shiner. "Did she cause any more commotion?"

"Believe it or not, Aphrodite did Psyche's

makeup for the wedding," I told him. "Not that she needed any," I added. "After the ceremony, Zeus hired the Invisible Nymph Band to play, and we danced all night."

"It sounds like a festive celebration," said Uncle Shiner.

"Well, it's not every day the god of love finds his soul mate," I said. "You know, Cupid's name means 'love' and Psyche's means 'soul.'"

"I know," said Shiner. "But your readers may not. I believe you should include that in your revision."

"Revision?" My heart sank. "You think the story needs more work?"

"All stories benefit from revision, Hades," Shiner said. "Homer revised *The Odyssey* countless times. I've made a few notes in the margins that may be helpful to you."

"Ah," I said. A few notes. That didn't sound too bad.

He gave the manuscript back to me, and I quickly flipped through the pages. I couldn't believe it! Uncle Shiner had scribbled all over my story!

"Thank you, Uncle Shiner," I said, trying to sound upbeat.

"Which myth will you tackle next, Hades?" asked the Cyclops.

"Theseus," I told him, trying to shove that whole revising conversation out of my mind. I opened *The Big Fat Book of Greek Myths.* "Take a look, Uncle Shiner. See what you think."

THE MORTAL THESEUS VOWED TO SLAY THE MINOTAUR, A MONSTER, HALF MAN AND HALF BULL. IN THE LABYRINTH MAZE, THESEUS FOUND THE MINOTAUR SURROUNDED BY PILES OF SKULLS AND BONES. HE SPRANG AT THE MONSTER AND KILLED HIM WITH HIS BARE HANDS.

Uncle Shiner looked up from the book. "Brave hero slays evil monster." He shrugged. "I fear there are quite a number of stories like that already, Hades."

"Not like this!" I told him. "Theseus went into the labyrinth, all right. But did he kill the Minotaur? Forget about it! The only thing Theseus did inside that maze was get good and lost."

"Hmmm, a flawed hero," said Shiner. "Go on."

"Theseus was tall and handsome," I said. "He had ambitions to be a hero, but there was one problem. He had the attention span of a gnat. The only reason anyone remembers his name to this day is that someone was always at his side, reminding him which quest he was on or which bad guy he was after."

Uncle Shiner's eye widened. "Is that right?"

I nodded. "And most of the time, that someone was me."

"It sounds like you have the start of a great adventure, Hades." Shiner stood up. "I won't keep you. The sooner you start writing the story of Theseus, the sooner I can read it." He gave me a big wink. He started to go and then turned back.

"One last question," he said. "How did Cyclops come out against Stinger?"

"On top." I smiled. "Eagle-Eye took the match."

King Hades's Quick-and-Easy Guide to the Myths

Let's face it, mortals, when you read the Greek myths, you sometimes run into long, unpronounceable names — names like *Aphrodite* and *Euridice* — names so long that just looking at them can give you a great big headache. Not only that, but sometimes you mortals call us by our Greek names and other times by our Roman names. It can get pretty confusing. But never fear! I'm here to set you straight with my quick-and-easy guide to who's who and what's what in the myths.

Alec (AL-eck) — see **Furies.**

ambrosia (am-BRO-zha) — food we gods must eat to stay young and good-looking for eternity.

Aphrodite (af-ruh-DIE-tee) — the goddess of love and beauty; one of the Twelve Power Olympians; rose fully-grown from the sea foam near the isle of Cythera; mother of Cupid; the Romans call her *Venus*.

Apollo (uh-POL-oh) — god of light, music, medicine, poetry, and the sun; one of the Twelve Power Olympians; son of Zeus and Leto. The Romans call him *Apollo*, too.

Asphodel Fields (AS-fo-del FEELDZ) — the large region of the Underworld where nothing grows except for a weedy gray-green plant; home to the ghosts of those who were not so good, but not so bad on earth.

Calydonian Boar (kal-uh-DOHN-ee-un) — a monstrous, fire-breathing wild boar sent by Artemis to punish the city of Calydon in northwestern Greece; said to run a wrestling academy.

Cerberus (SIR-buh-rus) — my fine, III-headed pooch; guard dog of the Underworld.

Charon (CARE-un) — river-taxi driver; ferries the living and the dead across the River Styx.

Cupid (KYOO-pid) — what the Romans call the little god of love; we Greeks prefer to call him *Eros*.

Cyclops (SIGH-klops) — any of three one-eyed giants; Lightninger, Shiner, and Thunderer, children of Gaia and Uranus, and uncles to us gods, are three *Cyclopes* (SIGH-klo-peez).

Cythera (si-THIR-uh) — A Greek island between the Peloponnese and Crete; Aphrodite rose from the sea and winds blew her to this island.

Daphne (DAF-nee) — a nymph chased by Apollo; her father, a river god, turned her into a laurel tree to save her from the god.

Delphi (DELL-fie) — an oracle in Greece on the southern slope of Mount Parnassus where a sibyl is said to predict the future.

Dodona (dough-DOUGH-nuh) — a land where talking oak trees reveal the will of Zeus.

drosis (DRO-sis) — short for *theoexidrosis* (thee-oh-ex-ih-DRO-sis), old Greek speak for "violent god sweat."

"Eagle-Eye" Cyclops (SIGH-klops) — another one of the Cyclopes; my favorite wrestling phenom.

Eurydice (yoo-RID-uh-see) — the wife of the great musician, Orpheus.

Furies (FYOOR-eez) — three winged immortals with red eyes and serpents for hair who pursue and punish wrongdoers, especially children who insult their mothers; their full names are *Tisiphone* (tih-ZIH-fuh-nee), *Megaera* (MEH-guh-ra), and *Alecto* (ah-LEK-toe), but around my palace, they're known as Tisi, Meg, and Alec.

Hades (HEY-deez) — Ruler of the Underworld, Lord of the Dead, King Hades, that's me. I'm also god of wealth, owner of all the gold, silver, and precious jewels in the Earth. The Romans call me *Pluto*.

Hyperion (hi-PEER-ee-un) — a way-cool Titan dude, once in charge of the sun and all the universe. Now retired, he owns a cattle ranch in the Underworld.

Hypnos (HIP-nos) — god of sleep; brother of Thanatos, god of death; son of Nyx, or night. Shhh! He's napping.

ichor (EYE-ker) — god blood

immortal (i-MOR-tuhl) — a being, such as a god or a monster, who will never die, like me.

Land of the Hyperborians (hi-per-BOR-ee-uns) — land in the far north, home to happy people who are always feasting and dancing.

Meg (MEG) — see **Furies.**

mortal (MOR-tuhl) — a being that must die. I hate to break this to you, but *you* are a mortal.

Mount Olympus (oh-LIM-pess) — the highest mountain in Greece; its peak is home to all the major gods, except for my brother Po and me.

nectar (NECK-ter) — what we gods like to drink; has properties that invigorate us and make us look good and feel godly.

nymph (NIMF) — any of the various female nature spirits.

oracle (OR-uh-kul) — a sacred place where seers or sibyls are said to foretell the future; the sibyls and their prophecies are also called oracles.

Orpheus (OR-fee-us) — legendary musician who married Eurydice.

Pegasus (PEG-uh-sus) — Medusa's white winged steed.

Persephone (per-SEF-uh-nee) — goddess of spring and Queen of the Underworld. The Romans call her *Proserpina*.

Psyche (SIGH-key) — a mortal princess loved by Cupid; her name means "soul."

Pygmalion (pig-MALE-yen) — a king who made a statue of a woman and fell in love with it.

Python (PIE-thon) — a huge serpent who guarded the oracle of Delphi; also known as a champion wrestler.

Roman numerals (ROH-muhn NOO-mur-uhlz) — what the ancients used instead of counting on their fingers. Makes you glad you live in the age of Arabic numerals and calculators, doesn't it?

I	1	XI	11	XXX	30
II	2	XII	12	XL	40
III	3	XIII	13	L	50
IV	4	XIV	14	LX	60
V	5	XV	15	LXX	70
VI	6	XVI	16	LXXX	80
VII	7	XVII	17	XC	90
VIII	8	XVIII	18	C	100
IX	9	XIX	19	D	500
X	10	XX	20	M	1000

Scorpion (SKOR-pee-un) — monstrous arachnid with venom in its tail; a wrestling phenom fated to be immortalized as a starry constellation.

sibyl (SIB-ul) — a mortal woman said to be able to foretell the future; a prophetess.

Tartarus (TAR-tar-us) — the deepest pit in the Underworld and home of the Punishment Fields, where burning flames and red-hot lava eternally torment the ghosts of the wicked.

Thalia (THA-lee-uh) — daughter of Zeus; the muse of comedy.

Thebes (THEEBZ) — city in Greece; home of Wrestle Dome.

Tisi (TIZ-ee) — see **Furies**.

Underworld (UHN-dur-wurld) — my very own kingdom, where the ghosts of dead mortals come to spend eternity.

Zephyr (ZEF-ur) — the West Wind.

Zeus (ZOOSE) —rhymes with *goose*, which pretty much says it all; last, and definitely least, my little brother, a major myth-o-maniac and a cheater, who managed to set himself up as Ruler of the Universe. The Romans call him *Jupiter*.

AN EXCERPT FROM

THE BIG FAT BOOK OF GREEK MYTHS

Cupid, the son of the goddess Aphrodite, was a handsome young god. It was his job to make people fall in love — anyone struck by one of his arrows would fall in love with the first person he or she saw.

Aphrodite was jealous of the beautiful mortal princess Psyche. Psyche's royal subjects loved her so much that they forgot to worship Aphrodite. So Aphrodite ordered her son to make Psyche fall in love with a horrible monster.

One night, Cupid snuck into Psyche's room to complete his task. But when he saw how beautiful Psyche was, Cupid was stunned. He accidentally scratched his arm with one of his own arrows and fell in love with her himself.

Although Psyche was beautiful, no one wanted to marry her. Her parents visited an oracle to find out why. The oracle told them that Psyche was fated to marry a monster and instructed them to leave her at the top of a mountain.

The West Wind carried Psyche away to a palace where she was waited on by invisible servants. At night, Cupid visited Psyche. He snuck into Psyche's room and promised to visit every night, but she must never try to see him.

But Psyche grew homesick. She convinced Cupid to let her sisters visit. Out of jealousy, her sisters said that Cupid must be a monster who wanted to eat her. They talked Psyche into peeking at her invisible suitor. When Psyche saw how handsome Cupid was, she was so shocked she dripped hot wax on him and woke him up.

Cupid immediately left, and the palace disappeared in a puff of smoke. Psyche searched the world for Cupid. She finally asked Aphrodite for help. Aphrodite was still angry with Psyche and gave her many tasks to complete.

When Cupid found out what was going on he persuaded Zeus to put a stop to it. Finally the great and powerful Zeus granted Psyche immortality so she could be with Cupid. Psyche became a goddess, and the two were married.

KATE MCMULLAN is the author of the chapter book series Dragon Slayers' Academy, as well as easy readers featuring Fluffy, the Classroom Guinea Pig. She and her illustrator husband, Jim McMullan, have created several award-winning picture books, including *I STINK!*, *I'M DIRTY!*, and *I'M BIG!* Her latest work is *SCHOOL! Adventures at Harvey N. Trouble Elementary* in collaboration with the famed *New Yorker* cartoonist George Booth. Kate and Jim live in Sag Harbor, NY, with two bulldogs and a mews named George.

GLOSSARY

ambitions (am-BISH-uhnz) — things you really want to do

chariot (CHA-ree-uht) — a small vehicle pulled by a horse, used in ancient times for battle or races

elaborate (ih-LAB-ur-it) — complicated and detailed

festive (FESS-tiv) — cheerful and lively

goblet (GOB-lit) — a tall drinking container with a stem and a base

hasty (HAY-stee) — too quick or hurried

lyre (LIRE) — a small, stringed, harp-like instrument played mostly in ancient Egypt, Israel, and Greece

perish (PER-ish) — to die or be destroyed

scheme (SKEEM) — a plan or plot for doing something

sibling (SIB-ling) — a brother or a sister

temple (TEM-puhl) — a building used for worship

temporary (TEM-puh-rer-ee) — something that only lasts for a short time

DISCUSS!

I. Why are Psyche's sisters so jealous of her? What are some good ways to handle jealousy?

II. Aphrodite doesn't make it easy for Psyche to see Cupid again. What do you think is the most difficult task on Aphrodite's list? Why?

III. Voice forbids Psyche from looking at him. If you were in Psyche's position, would you have peeked? Why or why not?

I. If you were Psyche, how would you have felt about being kidnapped and kept at Thunder Court? Write chapter XIII from her perspective.

II. Aphrodite gives Psyche a list of ten tasks she must complete in order to see Cupid again. Write your own list of impossible tasks.

III. Cupid is too embarrassed to let Psyche see him because he thinks she won't like him. Write about a time when you felt embarrassed or nervous. What happened?

MYTH-O-MANIA

MYTH-O-MANIA
HAVE A HOT TIME,
HADES!
KATE MCMULLAN

I

MYTH-O-MANIA
PHONE HOME,
PERSEPHONE!
KATE MCMULLAN

II

MYTH-O-MANIA
STOP THAT BULL,
THESEUS!
KATE MCMULLAN

V

MYTH-O-MANIA
KEEP A LID ON IT,
PANDORA!
DO NOT OPEN
KATE MCMULLAN

VI

READ THE WHOLE SERIES AND LEARN THE REAL STORIES!

III

IV

VII

VIII

THE FUN DOESN'T STOP HERE!

DISCOVER MORE:

Videos & Contests!
Games & Puzzles!
Heroes & Villains!
Authors & Illustrators!

@ WWW.CAPSTONEKIDS.COM

Find cool websites and more books like this one at WWW.FACTHOUND.COM. Just type in Book I.D. 9781434219855 and you're ready to go!